CAN'T TIE ME DOWN

SINCLAIR SISTERS 1

JANET ELIZABETH HENDERSON

First published in 2018 by Janet Elizabeth Henderson

© Janet Kortlever 2018

This edition 2019

This edition ISBN: 9780473461409

Text design by Vellum

Cover design by Janet Elizabeth Henderson

Editing by Liz Dempsey

PROLOGUE

Once upon a time, there were four Scottish sisters. These sisters grew up poor in the small town of Campbeltown, in the Mull of Kintyre (yes, Paul McCartney's Mull of Kintyre). When the eldest sister, Isobel, was sixteen, she fell pregnant to a boy who ran away as soon as he found out he was going to be a father. To make matters worse, Isobel's no-good, gambling and drinking tyrant of a father kicked her out of the house, leaving her to raise her baby alone.

But he misjudged his children, because Isobel wasn't alone.

As soon as her three younger sisters were able, they each left home and followed Isobel to the tiny village of Arness (which isn't that far from Campbeltown, but the houses were cheaper, so that's why Isobel moved there). Together, the four sisters worked to support each other and help Isobel raise her child.

One day, Isobel met a man and everything changed. This man was honorable and loved Isobel with all of his heart. He also ran a security company in London, and soon Isobel and her children (Isobel had a short marriage to a loser, which produced another child, but we won't talk about that here. Let's just say Isobel found it hard to keep her pants on, or to remember birth control!) moved away from Kintyre, to live happily ever after at the other end of Britain.

Which meant her three sisters were left alone and lost without her. They'd spent their entire adult lives working together to help Isobel, and now they had to find a purpose of their own. This book tells the story of one of those sisters, and how she managed to find her own version of a fairytale happily ever after.

But be warned, she's still a Sinclair sister, and those women don't do anything the easy way. Take the youngest of the four, Mairi, for example…

CHAPTER 1

It was an idyllic summer's day on Scotland's Kintyre peninsula. The sun was shining. The sky was blue. Gentle waves lapped at the shore beside the village of Arness. The Atlantic was calm, and through the morning haze, you could just about make out the coast of Ireland. The old gray stone buildings dotted around the village were postcard perfect, and there was purple heather growing on the bluff above the sea. Even the fields seemed greener than usual. Mairi Sinclair half expected a couple of Disney-style bluebirds to flutter past her bedroom window, carrying a sheet to hang on the line. It was perfect, until someone pounded on her front door.

"You need to get your bum out of bed and answer that," Agnes, Mairi's roommate and sister, snapped from the bathroom. "I'm getting ready for work."

And there went her chance at a lazy day in bed.

Reluctantly, Mairi threw back the bedcovers, just as there was another round of loud and impatient thumping at the front door.

"I'm coming," Mairi shouted, with quite a bit of irritation.

She threw on a pair of jeans, and a t-shirt with a photo of Princess Leia holding a blaster and the words *Don't Mess With a Princess* and ran, barefoot, for the door.

And that was when Mairi realized there was no way to salvage her potentially perfect day.

Because at eight thirty on a Saturday morning, she opened her front door to find Captain Kirk smiling at her—a five-foot-four Pakistani Captain Kirk.

"You are surprised." He beamed. "This is good."

Mairi blinked several times, but no, he was still there. "Amir?"

"Who else would it be on this fine Scottish morning?" He tugged at the hem of his gold captain's uniform.

"Amir? In Scotland? At my house?"

He opened his mouth to say something else, but Mairi needed a minute. She held up her hand. "Just a sec." And shut the door.

"Who was that?" One of Mairi's three older sisters, Agnes, was dressed for a shift working reception at a hotel in Campbeltown. She wore a navy pantsuit, black heels and a crisp white shirt. Her golden blonde hair was in a neat French knot, and her makeup was minimal. She looked every inch the hotel manager she aspired to be, and no doubt would be, once she'd passed her final exams. "Mairi, pay attention. Who's at the door?"

"Amir." Mairi wondered if more coffee would help her brain cope with finding one of her online boyfriends on her doorstep.

"Amir who?" Agnes headed for the kitchen alcove in their living area.

"He's an online boyfriend."

Agnes stopped dead and turned slowly toward her. "One of your geeks is here? In person?"

Mairi nodded.

"How does he know your address? I thought the agency you work with said those details would never get out. I thought all those guys were supposed to stay firmly online."

"Yeah." There was nothing else to say.

When she'd been a little girl, Mairi hadn't dreamed of growing up to become a fake online girlfriend to a bunch of socially inept men. Nope, she'd dreamed of castles and princess gowns and white knights. She nearly burst out laughing at the thought. It was so far from the truth it was almost hysterical. In all of Mairi's childhood dreams, *she'd* been the knight. And she hadn't been concerned with saving any foppish princes, either. No, Mairi had wanted to travel the world, seeking adventure and fighting dragons. Instead, she was stuck in Arness, sharing a tiny flat with her grumpy-arsed sister and dealing with an unwelcome Captain Kirk wannabe. This was not the happy ending she'd hoped for.

"Why is your online boyfriend here?" Agnes demanded, jarring Mairi out of her maudlin thoughts. "How did he get your address?"

"I don't know." And she didn't like it. There was a reason this job was perfect for her: it meant she got to keep men at arm's length. No chance of getting in too deep. No chance of falling in love and getting her heart broken by trusting the wrong man again.

"Well, ask him!" Agnes did that toe-tapping thing that Mairi hated, which was even more intimidating when she was dressed in her power suit.

With a scowl at her sister, Mairi turned and opened the door, to find a beaming Amir, exactly where she'd left him.

"Amir, how did you get my address?" *And why the hell did you fly all the way from Pakistan to visit me?* Didn't he realize their relationship was fake? He paid her weekly—that should have been a giant clue.

He looked slightly confused for a second, before the smile

appeared again. "This is a test, beautiful Mairi. I can answer this most easy of questions. You yourself posted the address on your website page. Now, I have something of the utmost importance to ask you." He rooted around in his trouser pocket.

"Just a minute." Mairi shut the door and looked at her sister. "He says I put the address on my page."

Agnes pointed at the laptop sitting on their tiny dining table, and Mairi headed toward it. A few keystrokes later, and she was looking at a notice she had definitely *not* posted.

I'm tired of being single. As much as I've enjoyed being a girl-friend to all of you, I now want more. I want marriage and a family. I want my own happily ever after. The only problem is that I've managed to fall a little bit in love with all of my wonderful boyfriends. So, I'm giving you a challenge—a quest. Whoever gets to Arness, Scotland, first and wins my heart in person will win my hand in marriage. So, scale the walls of my castle, woo me with your knightly skills, and save this fair maiden from a life of loneliness and heartache. May the best man win!

It was followed by her street address, and a link to a Facebook page called *Mairi's Wedding Challenge*, where supposedly she was going to give updates as things progressed. The message ended with a Photoshopped image of her as Rapunzel, leaning out of a tower and gazing wistfully into the distance, presumably for her prince.

"I'm going to vomit." Mairi bent over and put her head between her knees.

"Get up." Agnes smacked the back of her head. "Get on that site and delete the post. Write something that tells all those sad sacks you talk to that this is a mistake."

There was a sharp rap at the door. "Mairi, my love?" Amir called.

Mairi swallowed hard and brought up the login page for the Girlfriend site. She typed furiously. Three times. And then panicked. "I'm locked out. I'm emailing the owner." She opened her emails and typed. The answer was instantaneous. "Oh no." Mairi moaned.

"What?" Agnes peered over her shoulder.

"They've been hacked." Mairi resisted the urge to thump her head on the table. It wouldn't help anyway. "They're locked out of their own site and can't change the message either."

"Mairi, my little Scottish flower, open the door. I have something important to ask you." Amir's voice floated into the room.

"You need to deal with that." Agnes pointed at the door. "Now."

"Fine." Dragging her feet, Mairi went to their front door and opened it.

No Amir. A throat cleared. She looked down. He was on one knee, holding out a ring box.

"Mairi, my love," he said solemnly, "I must be asking you the most serious of questions. I wish for you to be my wife. Together we will explore strange new worlds and seek out new life and new civilizations. I wish to boldly go where no man has gone before. I wish to be your husband."

Mairi shut the door and leaned back against it.

"This isn't good," she said to her sister.

"You think?" Agnes glared at her.

"Mairi," Amir called, "is that a yes?"

"Heads up, there's a Wookiee coming this way."

Keir jerked up at his fellow mechanic's words and hit his head on the underside of the car hood. "What the hell are you talking about now?" he asked his fifty-two-year-old second-career apprentice.

Hamish pointed, and Keir looked through the open garage doors. Sure enough, there was a guy in a huge hairy costume, sauntering across what passed for the main street in Arness. Keir stepped back from the car, grabbed a rag and wiped the oil off his hands.

"Can I help you with something?" he asked the Wookiee.

"Argharghah!" the Wookiee said.

There was a split second where Keir wondered if he'd inhaled too many petrol fumes and this was the result. Then a short guy wearing jeans, and a t-shirt that said, *Physicists Do It at the Speed of Light*, ran across the road to join the Wookiee.

"Ignore him," the short guy said. "He likes to think he's being authentic. He won't talk anything but Wookiee while he's in his Chewbacca costume. He's a *Star Wars* purist."

The big, furry guy opened his mouth and warbled.

"No." The little guy frowned, "I'm not going to translate for you. Every man for himself." He turned back to Keir. "We're looking for Mairi Sinclair. The woman in the shop told us she lives over here, in the apartment upstairs. Do we get there through the garage, or is there another entrance?"

Keir put down the rag, folded his arms over his black tank, making sure they noted his muscles and tattoos, and stepped into their space.

"What do you want with Mairi?" The Wookiee opened his mouth to answer, and Keir held up a hand. "In English."

"She's going to be my wife," the little guy said with pride. The Wookiee roared with what was clearly a protest. The other guy scowled up at him. "How are you going to propose? She doesn't speak Wookiee. You shot yourself in the foot wearing that costume. It's not my fault I'm going to win."

Keir uncrossed his arms and pressed his fingers to his temples. "Win? What the hell are you two talking about?"

The smaller guy dug into his pocket and came out with a phone. He flicked at the screen before turning it to Keir. He found himself looking at a website called Girlfriends for Hire. And there was a photo of Mairi, smiling out at him from a fake medieval tower and telling him that she specialized in online relationships with geeks. Geeks? Keir shook his head and kept reading. Under her photo was an updated message to her "men." One that obviously hadn't been written by Mairi. For a start, it said she wanted to get married. If this was the real deal, he'd eat an oily rag and wash it down with antifreeze.

"Mairi wants a husband," the little guy said. "She challenged her online boyfriends to woo her." He looked up at the Wookiee. "Do people still say woo?"

The Wookiee shook his head and made some noise.

"Wait a minute," Keir said, as the words sank in. "Why the hell would you want a girlfriend who only exists online?"

"Hiring an online girlfriend is a sensible alternative to being alone forever." The little guy sounded like he actually believed what he was saying. "Most of us work in male-dominated industries, like tech or research. Or we live in isolated areas. We don't have a lot of time to meet women, and most of us don't have a clue what to do with them when we do. That's how we ended up on the Girlfriend site. For a small weekly fee, you get to interact with a woman who helps you learn how to, well, interact with women. It gives you confidence. Practice. That sort of thing. It's all aboveboard. Strictly no nudity." He looked so disappointed about the lack of nudity that Keir almost laughed.

The Wookiee started gesturing and making Wookiee noises.

"Yeah," the little guy said, "and it means we can get people off our backs about relationships. My parents totally stopped setting me up with random women once they'd Skyped with Mairi."

Keir stared at the two of them for a minute, letting the explanation sink in. A campervan rolled past the garage and came to a stop outside the village shop. Two more guys got out. One wore jeans, and a black t-shirt, and looked normal; the other wore a short-sleeved checked shirt, with a clashing tie. There were pens in his shirt pocket. It didn't take a PhD in logic to figure out Keir was looking at yet another "boyfriend."

"How many of you are there?" Keir asked.

The short guy checked with the Wookiee. "About thirty, we think. Mairi capped the number because she wanted to spend quality time with each of us."

More likely, she capped the number because that was the most her fluffy little brain could cope with. "And you all know each other?"

They nodded in unison, before the little guy said, "She specializes in geeks. And being geeks, we formed an online forum to talk about her. Kind of like a boyfriend support group, or a Mairi fan club."

"You don't care that she's fake-dating all of you?" Keir said.

"We're smart guys. We knew it was a business deal. And then she changed everything with her declaration. Now, the boyfriends are at war, and the forum has been disbanded until one of us wins her heart for real."

"You're serious. This isn't some kind of nerdy cosplay event? You really want to marry Mairi?" Keir glanced around, wondering if someone was going to jump out and shout "punk'd" at him.

"Dude, have you seen Mairi? She's hot, and she's a fangirl."

"Fangirl?"

He received a look of derision. "She can geek with the best of them. She knows the names of all the *Star Trek* TOS episodes, and she understands the wrongness of Jar Jar Binks."

The Wookiee said something, and the little guy nodded. "That's true. She doesn't know anything about anime. It's her one flaw."

Keir pinched the bridge of his nose. It was going to be a long, long day.

"I have a couple of questions," Hamish said from beside Keir. The older man folded his arms over the shirt and tie he insisted on wearing to work every day and frowned at the Wookiee. "In this internet message Mairi wrote, she told you to make your best effort to romance her. Do you really think dressing like a scabby bear and yawning your words is your A-game?" He turned to the little guy. "And for your information, doing *it* at the speed of light isn't something you should advertise, son."

Keir groaned.

"What am I going to do?" Mairi said. "I need a plan. And a rope ladder. Amir's blocked our entrance, and I can't use the stairs down into the garage or I'll have to deal with Keir. If I had a rope ladder, I could go out the bedroom window and make a run for it."

"You're acting like you really are Rapunzel," Agnes said. "Get a grip. You can't run. You need to get online and sort this mess out before the rest of your fake boyfriends turn up." She stalked to the living room window, which overlooked the Arness main street. "Oh, this can't be good."

"What can't?" Mairi rushed to her side, and together they peeked out from behind the ancient net curtains that had come with the flat. There was a Wookiee standing in the middle of the road, staring up at their windows. "Crap, that's Jonas."

He waved, and she waved back. It was all a bit surreal. As she watched, two men came out of the village shop and climbed into a campervan. Twin men. "Oh no." Mairi groaned. "That's the Dawson twins." She watched as they maneuvered the van into the parking lot behind the shop.

"You're the girlfriend of twins?"

"Fake girlfriend!" Mairi frowned at her sister. "Why can't anyone remember the fake part?"

"But brothers? Is that even legal?"

"It doesn't matter if it's legal or not. It's fake!" Mairi stomped away from the window. "And to be fair, only one of them is a geek. The other one just talks to me for a laugh. He has plenty of real girlfriends."

"Oh, well then, that makes it okay." Agnes perched on the edge of their wobbly dining table. "As long as it's fake."

That was it. Mairi'd had enough. She stood in front of her sister, hands on hips, and glared. "You're being judgmental? Really? When my job helps pay for your study?"

"You're right. I'm sorry." Agnes didn't look even slightly contrite. "But twins?"

"Get a grip. It's fake. It's all fake. I don't even like bloody *Star Trek*!"

"Mairi," Amir called. "I am still waiting for your most glorious of answers."

Mairi stared at the ceiling while she counted to ten. The rope ladder idea was still looking pretty good. She could climb out the window, hitch a lift to Campbeltown and then catch a bus to London. Surely her sister Isobel would put her up for a week or two until this blew over?

"I know what you're thinking," Agnes said. "You can't dump this on Isobel's doorstep. She needs time to get used to living with Callum. She deserves to be happy. She's spent her life sorting out other people's messes. You need to deal with this on your own."

Mairi sighed. Unfortunately, Agnes was right. Although… Isobel was living with a guy who was a partner in an international security company. A security company with a genius hacker on board. Mairi perked right up.

"I could call Isobel, though, and ask her to get someone to look into who hacked my web page."

Agnes frowned as she thought about it. "Don't you think that's a bit presumptuous? Asking favors from Callum's business when Isobel's relationship with him is so new."

"It's their honeymoon phase. This is *exactly* the time to get her to ask him for a favor. Right now, he'd do anything to get her to drop her pants. Not that it takes much." Their eldest sister was a bit loose with her favors. Unlike Mairi, who was nursing a born-again hymen.

"You could offer to pay," Agnes said.

They looked at each other and burst into hysterical laughter. Offer was all they could do. Every penny the sisters made had either gone into Agnes' degree or had been used to help Isobel pay off her ex-husband's debt.

"I'm calling Isobel," Mairi said, when she'd calmed down a little. "I have to do something. If she can get someone to undo the mess the hacker's made, and get me back on my web page, that would be great. I need to tell everyone that I don't want a husband. I can't let these guys turn up expecting me to marry one of them. I have thirty online boyfriends—what if they all turn up? What if they camp here forever? You can't underestimate the stubbornness of a geeky man. They'll view this like an online game and keep playing until one of them gets the highest score. Me!"

"Calm down," Agnes said helpfully.

"Calm down?" Mairi glared at her sister. "This is a crisis

situation. These guys don't think like you and me. They think like Gandalf and Luke Skywalker! You read the website message. They think they're on some freaking quest to vanquish evil and win the fair maiden. Before you know it, they'll be out there, dueling with lightsabers and mocking each other's costumes. Trust me. I need to deal with this now, before it gets a whole lot worse."

"Hey, gorgeous," a deep male voice said. "I hear you're looking for a husband."

Both women squealed and spun toward the voice. Keir was standing in the doorway that led down to the garage, grinning like an idiot.

"See what I mean?" Mairi shouted at her sister. "It just got worse!"

CHAPTER 2

There was no denying that Mairi Sinclair did it for Keir. With her wild, wavy red hair and her blazing green eyes, she exuded passion with every movement she made. He loved her quirky, offbeat way of thinking, her petite height and her generous curves. In fact, the only things he didn't like about Mairi were that she held a grudge, and she wouldn't give him a second chance.

"Mairi!" someone shouted from outside the front door. "Are you okay?"

There was a thud, followed by a howl of pain. Mairi rolled her eyes and stomped to the door. She threw it open to reveal yet another guy in costume.

"Amir, I'm fine. Don't try to break down the door. You'll only hurt yourself." She sounded so long-suffering that Keir couldn't help but laugh. Which earned him frowns from the sisters, before their attention returned to the *Star Trek* impersonator.

"You screamed." Amir rubbed his shoulder and frowned over at Keir. "There is a man in your apartment."

"He's only my landlord, and right now, I have to go deal with him. I think you should leave." She shut the door.

"But you have not answered my question," he called.

Mairi growled and threw the door open again. "The answer is no, Amir. Thank you for asking." She slammed it shut in the poor guy's face.

"This is not the last time I will ask," he shouted. "Never give up, never surrender!"

"You're a *Star Trek* officer," Mairi shouted back. "That's *Galaxy Quest*."

"What are you doing?" Agnes demanded. "Is it really that important that he gets his quotes right? There's a bigger picture to deal with here."

"I know. I know. I can't help it. I've been studying up on this stuff for three years." Mairi tapped her head. "Sometimes, I wonder if there's room left in my brain for anything else."

Keir started to laugh again, and that drew more scowls from the sisters. "What? It's funny."

"Why are you here?" Mairi strode toward him. "We talked about this. Rental law states that you aren't allowed to enter your rental property without the permission of the tenants. Which is never going to happen."

Agnes let out a sigh. "I invite him in all the time."

"Your permission doesn't count," Mairi snapped.

"Dual tenancy, remember?" Agnes said. "Plus, I'm older. I'm the one in charge here. My permission is totally the one that counts."

Mairi dismissed her sister's logic with a wave of her hand. "Get out of my flat," she ordered Keir.

He pointed at his motorcycle-boot-clad feet. "I'm still in the hallway. No laws have been broken here. And to be fair, I've only ever come into the flat when Agnes invited me, or when I've needed to deal with an emergency situation. Like the time you left the bath running, flooded the flat and brought down the garage ceiling. Or the time you left a pot on the stove, went to Campbeltown and the building nearly burned down. Or the time—"

She held up a hand to stop him. "Yeah, yeah, you're a selfless superhero. That still doesn't tell me why you're here."

"I thought that'd be obvious." He couldn't help but grin at her. Sparring with Mairi was the only way she let him get close to her these days, and a man had to take what he could get. "I'm here to offer a solution to your problem."

"Unless you know how to un-hack a website and fix the message I supposedly posted—with Rapunzel illustrations— then you're no use to me."

She showed more disgust over the Rapunzel image than she did about the men camped outside her door. Keir shook his head in an attempt to get out of Mairi Land and back into reality.

"I've been talking to a couple of your boyfriends." And didn't that sentence just stick in his throat. "They're here for the long haul. Nobody's going home until you're off the market. This situation isn't going to disappear when you get rid of the post on your web page."

As if on cue, a car horn that played the first few bars of the *Star Wars* theme tune blasted from the street below them.

"And you think you know how to get rid of these guys?" she scoffed at him.

"Aye, I do. All you need to do to make them leave is get married." He spread his arms wide and gave her a lazy smile. "I'm offering myself up as the sacrificial lamb."

The two sisters gave him identical open-mouthed looks.

"Are you out of your mind?" Mairi snapped. "I don't want to marry anyone. Especially you. Go away. This isn't funny. Go amuse yourself somewhere else."

She shoved his chest to get him out of the doorway. It was

like a butterfly trying to move a gorilla. He didn't even sway. All he did was feel the heat of her touch sear through his shirt and make his skin tingle. He had to clench his hands tight to stop from reaching for her.

"Think about it," Keir said. "We get married, they go away, and then we get divorced." The last bit was a lie. If he managed to legally tie Mairi to him, there was no way he was letting her go.

"Over my dead body." She shoved him again and made that cute little growling noise when he didn't budge.

"It will make all your problems disappear," he said.

"Only to replace them with another six-foot-two problem." She put her fists on her hips. "Will you just leave?"

"Sure." He took his own sweet time over pushing away from the doorframe. "But the offer still stands. I'm sure we could make the most of a wedding night, sweet cheeks, so it wouldn't be a total loss." He watched her flush and knew she was remembering the one amazing night they'd had together —before he'd blown everything they'd been building together. "Think about it. You know where to find me when you make up your mind."

He turned and sauntered for the stairs, unsurprised to hear the door slam behind him.

"It isn't a bad idea," Agnes said, as Mairi stared at the closed door.

"Are you out of your mind too? It's a terrible idea."

The words came out with far more of a quaver than Mairi intended. Keir did that to her. He destabilized her foundations. He was her kryptonite. Around him, she was weak. She hung her head in disgust. Three years dealing with geeks, and even her private thoughts were peppered with comic book metaphors.

"You'd rather marry a guy you don't know, to get out of this mess?" Agnes said.

"I'm not getting married at all. Especially if my options are a bunch of guys I'm paid to date and an ex-convict who lives to drive me insane."

"Don't call him that. He made a mistake. We all do."

"My mistakes don't send me to prison."

"That's only by the grace of God." Agnes picked up her briefcase. "You said it yourself, these guys aren't going to go away. Keir's idea has merit. You go through with the ceremony. You show the geeks the certificate, and then you divorce Keir."

"And then what?" Mairi threw herself onto their lumpy secondhand sofa. "If I marry someone, I lose my job. It's not like I can carry on being a fake girlfriend when I have a husband at home."

Agnes' face softened. "Maybe it's time to find a new job."

"Where?" Mairi spread her arms wide. "Arness has two businesses. We live above one, and the local dragon runs the other." She was *not* working in the local shop. Dragons were meant to be slain. She sure as hell wasn't going to let one boss her around.

Agnes bit her bottom lip and looked unsure of herself for a second. "Maybe it's time to leave Arness. Once I get my final exam results, I'm applying for the management job at the Ferguson hotel. I'm bound to get it. I know that hotel better than the owner. It's a good salary, and I can finance you while you figure out what to do next. It's the least I can do. You've carried the burden while I studied."

"I can't think about leaving Arness right now." And to be honest, just saying the words made Mairi feel sick with anxiety. Arness was pretty much all she knew, and the big wide world suddenly seemed pretty damn terrifying. She snorted. So much for being a knight set on adventure. She took a deep breath and faced her sister. "I need to get rid of my fake boyfriends, then I'll think about the future."

"Honey, the future is already here. It's beating down your door." Agnes cast a glance over her shoulder. "Literally."

"I know, I know." The rope ladder idea was looking better every minute. "Go. You don't want to be late."

There was a scraping noise just outside their front door, and then it crashed open. Their middle sister stumbled in, apologizing to Amir, who was now sitting on the top step outside their apartment, cradling his hand against his chest.

"Sorry again," she said. "I didn't mean to step on you. I really hope your fingers are okay. Do you want me to get some ice?"

"No." Amir sounded strained. "I am fine. Thank you."

"I really am sorry." Donna flushed red and shut the door. "I think I broke his fingers." She bit her bottom lip. "Should I call an ambulance or something?"

"You dingbat," Agnes said, with a shake of her head.

"Don't worry about Amir," Mairi said. "He works in medical research. I'm sure he knows what to do about broken fingers."

"Okaaaay." Donna didn't look so sure. "I got your text. What's the emergency?"

Mairi glared at Agnes. "You sent out the Bat-Signal for Donna?"

Agnes rolled her eyes. "Like I'm going to leave you alone with that." She pointed at the door. "Somebody needs to babysit your backside and make sure you don't do something dumb. Or make a run for it."

"Is anybody going to tell me what's going on?" Donna asked as the music from *Psycho* suddenly blasted from her handbag.

"You want to answer that first?" Agnes said.

"Nope." Donna shook her head. "It's the 'Lord of the Manor'. He can do without me for an hour. I swear there are days when I feel more like his slave than his housekeeper. I've had enough of his bad attitude for today. His calls can go unanswered. I'm taking a stand against tyranny."

"By hiding?" Agnes cast a skeptical glance at Mairi as Donna deflated.

"Yeah." Donna slumped onto the other end of the sofa. "Who's Amir, anyway? Why is he sitting outside your door? And why is the street full of men wearing Fozzie Bear costumes?"

"That's a Wookiee costume. Not a Muppet." Mairi sighed. Didn't her sisters know anything?

"Yeah," Agnes said drolly. "Let's focus on getting the costumes right." She turned to Donna. "The men are here for Mairi. She gets to pick one and live happily ever after."

"They're my fake boyfriends," Mairi corrected.

"But they want to be her husband," Agnes added.

"The fake boyfriends are here? In real life?" Donna's eyes grew even wider. "Wait a minute? Did you say husband?"

"Aye," Agnes said with a grin. "Mairi's getting married."

"Am not!" Mairi shouted.

"Are too!" Amir shouted through the door.

Mairi groaned, Agnes started to laugh, and Donna just looked confused—as *Psycho* music once again filled the room.

CHAPTER 3

By early evening, it became apparent that the men weren't going anywhere. There were half a dozen motorhomes parked behind the village shop, and the grass expanse between the main street and the cliff edge had been turned into a campground. All day long, Mairi's online boyfriends had been turning up, in the hope of marrying her. She supposed she should have been flattered, but mainly she felt cornered.

Thumping at the front door dragged her attention from the window overlooking Arness' nameless main street.

"Open up," Agnes shouted. "My hands are full."

Mairi put the bowl of popcorn she'd been eating down beside the armchair, which she'd dragged over to face the window, and went to open the door. She was confronted by several bouquets of flowers, with legs.

"Agnes?"

A vase was thrust at her. "Don't just stand there. Take some of this."

Mairi had no choice but to take the flowers Agnes handed

her. "Where did you get these?" she said, as she backed into the flat under the weight of the bouquets.

"These are some of the flowers your men have had delivered to you," Agnes grumbled, following her. "They were left downstairs in the garage."

"Why didn't you get Keir to bring them up?"

"She did," Keir snapped, as he followed Agnes up the stairs, his arms full of yet more flowers.

With matching frowns, Agnes and Keir put the displays on the floor, as their tiny table was already filled with the ones Mairi had set down.

"Have you been hiding in here all day?" Agnes gave her a disapproving look.

"Not hiding, no. Assessing the situation and formulating a response." Mairi grinned. That sounded damn good. But from Agnes' frown, she wasn't impressed.

Mairi surveyed the blooms as the room filled with their perfume. She'd never seen so many flower arrangements, outside of the church fair.

"That's a lot of flowers," she said.

"There's more downstairs." Keir folded his arms, making his muscles bulge.

It was hard to stop her eyes from straying to his arms. Part of her wanted to grip those muscles tight, while her tongue traced the Celtic knot tattoo that trailed over his shoulder and disappeared under his shirt. She'd seen him without his shirt. She knew that tattoo went across his pec and down to abs that would make any grown woman drool.

She felt her cheeks flush at the thought of touching a shirtless Keir. Then she saw his knowing look and forced a glare. She might enjoy looking, but she sure as hell wasn't going to touch. Never again. His cocked eyebrow said otherwise. It, along with the smug little smile playing around his full, biteable lips, was a challenge. One she wasn't going to take.

She pointed at him. "You can leave now."

And, of course, he ignored her. "According to one of your men, you told them all that they should send flowers to a woman they're interested in. Apparently, it was only one piece of the advice you gave them on how to romance a woman."

Oh, that's not good. Mairi's mind rushed over all the things she'd told the boys under the guise of 'sage dating advice from a real woman.' She felt the color drain from her face. Yeah, there were some things she maybe *shouldn't* have told them.

"What did you do?" Agnes did that toe-tapping thing again.

"Nothing to worry about." Mairi mentally crossed her fingers and thought of the most likely reason for the flowers. "I saw an article in *Cosmo* that I thought the boys would find helpful, and I passed it on to them."

"Which article, exactly?" Agnes' toe was tapping faster now.

"It's no big deal. It was called 'Top Ten Romantic Gestures for Men.' See? Flowers are one of the gestures. That's it." *Move along. Nothing to see here.*

It was clear they weren't buying it.

Keir considered the flowers. "What were the other nine?"

Mairi chewed at her bottom lip while she thought about it. "Scented candles, chocolates, love notes, chivalrous gestures, meaningful songs, intimate dinners for two, foot rubs and grand gestures…" She trailed off, hoping they didn't realize that she'd only listed nine in total.

"Okay." Agnes put her hands on her hips. "A few extra meals and some scented candles are okay. We can live with those. I'm a bit worried about the grand gestures, but honestly, how creative can a bunch of geeks get?"

"Not so fast," Keir said. "That was only nine. What's the last one?"

Mairi glared at him. He was *not* helping. "Why are you still here, anyway? Remember the rule? No entering our flat without an invitation."

"I invited him," her traitor sister said, "now spit out number ten."

There was no avoiding Agnes' determined glare. Mairi could feel her cheeks beginning to heat again, so she muttered the words, before turning back to the flowers. "Aren't they gorgeous?" she said loudly.

"I didn't catch that," Agnes said. "Don't make me sit on you until you tell us properly."

"Fine!" Mairi threw herself back onto the sofa and folded her arms. "Number ten was 'the gift that keeps on giving.'"

"And that is?" Agnes said through gritted teeth, which was a sure sign that violence was about to occur.

"Oh hell." Mairi let out a breath. "*Cosmo* said that a cheeky gift would be welcomed after the couple got to know each other a little."

"I am this close to sitting on you and torturing you until you spit the damn thing out." Agnes took a step toward her.

"Don't! It's sex toys. Okay? Happy now?"

Agnes gaped at her.

Keir groaned. "They're going to send you sex toys?"

"Only if we get to that stage." Mairi looked at the flowers. "Toys were number ten on the list. And let's face it, where would they get them around here? You need to be realistic. You can order flowers to be delivered, maybe even chocolate, but sex toys? I don't think we need to worry."

Agnes pinched the bridge of her nose. "Have you told the men this is all a mistake?"

"Not exactly. First, I called Isobel, only to find out that Callum has taken her and the kids to Disneyland Paris, as a honeymoon treat—although, seeing as they haven't had a wedding, I'm not sure you can call it a honeymoon."

They glared at her with clear impatience.

"Moving on," Mairi said. "I didn't feel right asking to speak to their company hacker, so instead, I spent the day trying to get onto my web page myself. Turns out I have no hacking skills and the site is still locked down tight.

"After that, I spent some time trying to post a rebuttal on the fake Mairi's Wedding Facebook page, but I've been banned. I created another identity so I could post under that, but whoever was running the page realized it was me and banned that one too. So, then I started my own Facebook page, called Mairi Will Never Get Married, and posted a rebuttal on there. Unfortunately, nobody knows the page exists, so I don't think the guys have seen my message."

Keir and Agnes just stared at her, and there was a couple of minutes of awkward silence.

"It's a miracle you can walk and talk at the same time," Agnes said, with a shake of her head.

Mairi ignored her. "Oh, and when Donna left, she told some of the guys that they shouldn't be here. So, word did start to get out about this being a mistake."

Keir did that snorting thing that was supposed to be taken as a mocking laugh. Instead, all it did was remind her that all men were pigs.

"You can leave now," Mairi told him. "Thanks for the delivery."

He smirked at her, and Mairi felt her irritation rise. Keir was good at that. Around him, she was always annoyed.

"Donna told them to leave?" Agnes said. "Our sister Donna? The sister who was so worried she'd hurt the feelings of the Jehovah's Witnesses who turned up on her doorstep, that she ended up spending a weekend at a religious retreat? The same sister who is a member of the Bacon of the Month Club, because she couldn't say no to the telemarketer, even though she's vegetarian? The woman who works at a job she didn't apply for, and isn't qualified for, because she turned up at the owner's house at the wrong time, and he told her the job was hers? *That* sister told your men to leave town?"

"You get tiny wee lines between your eyebrows when you're being sarcastic." Mairi pointed at Agnes' face. "Now that you're thirty, you might want to watch that." The lines deepened, and Mairi shook her head. "Fine, don't take my advice, but I hear lines are easier to avoid getting than they are to get rid of."

Agnes made a low growling sound that would have been scary if Mairi hadn't heard it all before. Agnes took a step toward Mairi, but Keir's hand snapped out to restrain her.

"You know," he said to Mairi, "my offer to help still stands. We can be married in the morning."

She blinked at him. He was the burr under her saddle. The pebble in her shoe. The thorn in her side. Why he'd come back to Arness, she really didn't know. It wasn't like there was enough business to keep him here. His garage only survived because he gave a discount for cars sent to him from Campbeltown. It would be so much better for them both if he moved himself, and his garage, over there.

"I have a plan," Mairi told Agnes, ignoring the groan she got in reply. "I'm going to hold a meeting, with a whiteboard and bullet points. These guys understand bullet points. I'm going to list all the reasons why I don't want to get married and make it clear that this is the sick hoax of a bored hacker. All I need is a hall for the meeting, and a whiteboard."

Keir leaned a shoulder against the wall, his ankles crossed, and his hands in his jeans pockets. He was amused.

Which was really annoying, because she wasn't being funny. Agnes let out another growl, stomped to the living room window and threw it wide open. She put her fingers to her lips and let out a shrill whistle. Silence descended over Arness' main street.

"Get over here," she shouted. "Mairi has an announcement."

Mairi grabbed her sister's suit jacket and tried to pull her away from the window. "What are you doing? I don't even have a whiteboard."

The look Agnes gave her made her think that her sister was considering throwing her out of the window, as a sacrifice to the hordes.

"Fine. I'll talk. But this isn't going to go well without visual aids." Mairi knew her men. They needed diagrams.

She heard murmuring and shuffling from the street below and peeked out from behind the curtain. Sure enough, the men were gathering, just as Agnes had ordered them to. She had a gift for bossing people around. Mairi had long thought it was because in Agnes' head there wasn't even a sliver of doubt that she was in charge.

"Get on with it," Agnes snapped.

"I'm thinking," Mairi snapped back.

She heard a deep chuckle behind her and chose to ignore Keir. Once she'd dealt with the boyfriends, she'd deal with him.

"Okay." She took a deep breath, plastered a smile on her face and stepped in front of the open window.

There was a cheer and a round of applause. Mairi grinned at the familiar faces and waved. She felt like a celebrity. Or royalty. It was actually kind of cool.

"Stop playing to the crowd," Agnes snapped. "Tell them this is all a mistake."

Mairi cleared her throat, motioned for silence, and was

surprised when she got it. "There's been a mistake," she shouted so that everyone could hear. "My web page was hacked. Someone else wrote the message about me wanting to get married. It's all a lie. I don't want to get married. You can all go home now."

There was silence, and then they started chuckling. Mairi frowned at them. "I'm serious. I'm not getting married. I don't want a husband. This is all a mistake."

"We read your Facebook posts, Mairi. You told us there that you'd say this if you weren't impressed by our efforts to woo you," somebody shouted. "We know this is a ploy to weed out the boyfriends who aren't serious."

Mairi squinted in the direction of the voice. "John?"

"Hi, Mairi," he shouted back.

She took a second to let it sink in that the guy had come all the way from Australia for this fiasco.

"I have nothing to do with that Facebook page. It's run by the same person who hacked me. You need to trust what I'm saying and go home."

There was more laughter.

"I'm being serious," she shouted, feeling frustrated. She turned to Agnes. "They don't believe me. I told you this would happen. I need a whiteboard."

"Get out of my way." Agnes pushed her aside. "Listen up," she shouted. "You need to go home. Mairi was hacked. She won't be marrying any of you."

"Don't worry," somebody shouted, "we'll step up our game. You'll be impressed with what we have planned. Isn't that right, lads?"

There was a loud cheer.

"You know," Keir said, "I can stop this in a split second. All you have to do is agree to marry me."

"I'd rather stick a fork in my eye," Mairi told him, as the men outside began to chant her name.

Agnes gave up and slammed the window shut, then pulled the curtains tight. "I always wondered what mass hysteria looked like. Now I know."

"I told you they wouldn't listen," Mairi said. "They need proof."

"And how are you going to give them proof?" Agnes demanded.

"I haven't figured that part out yet. I only got as far as bullet points."

There was a noise at the front door, and they turned to see a piece of paper slip under it. Keir shook his head before bending to pick it up. And yes, Mairi checked out his backside. It wasn't like she could help it. It was right there, blocking her view of the door.

Keir unfolded the paper and read aloud. "'Roses are red, violets are blue, my dearest Mairi, please say "I do." Signed, Kevin Partridge, PhD.'" Keir's lips twitched, and his eyes sparkled as he looked at her. "I'm guessing the PhD isn't in poetry."

"Give me that." Mairi snatched it from his hand.

"We need to call the police," Agnes said. "Have them get rid of the guys."

"They won't," Keir said. "Edna at the shop is happy to have them here, and she gave permission for them to camp on her land. They aren't breaking any laws or causing any trouble. The police can't do anything. But I can." He started humming the 'Wedding March', and Mairi's fist actually tingled at the thought of thumping him in the stomach. Although the blow would probably cause more damage to her hand than to his abs.

"This is serious," Agnes said. "I have to go to Glasgow this evening, to sit exams tomorrow. I'll be gone all week. I can't leave you here to deal with this alone. What if one of them takes things too far? How do we know you'll be safe here?"

She nodded, as though coming to a decision. "You need to come with me."

"No!" The last thing Mairi wanted was to share a tiny room in the university halls of residence with Agnes during exam time. Apart from the fact she'd likely kill her sister if they were living in such close quarters, these exams were important. Agnes had been working toward this for ten years. Mairi wasn't going to blow it for her. "I'll be fine here, and I promised Gladys I'd take her to her chemo appointment tomorrow. Don't worry. I know these guys. They're harmless."

"You don't know them," Agnes said. "You know their online personas. You don't know anything about them in real life. What if one of them is violent? Or can't take no for an answer? It isn't safe. I'm sure Gladys will understand if you don't make it this time."

"It's her last appointment. I can't miss it because there's a bunch of harmless guys parked outside our door."

"Harmless? You don't know that. You only know what they show you online. We're isolated here. We don't even have any neighbors to rely on. The garage is empty all night, and the shop over the road shuts at eight. The nearest person to hear you scream is Old Man McIntosh, and he's deaf as a post. No, if they aren't going to leave, you need to come to Glasgow with me. It's the safest thing to do."

Mairi opened her mouth to argue, because she would rather walk barefoot on Lego than go with her sister, but Keir beat her to it.

"I can stay here and watch her while you're gone."

Mairi's eyes snapped to his face in time to see a slow, wicked smile appear.

"Thank you, Keir, that's a weight off my mind," Agnes said at the same time as Mairi screamed, "Hell no!"

Keir just looked smug.

CHAPTER 4

"I don't know what you're trying to achieve," Mairi said. "But whatever it is, it isn't going to happen. You should go home. I don't need, or want, you here."

"Thanks for clearing that up." Keir dumped his overnight bag on the end of the single bed that Agnes used. "I promised Agnes I'd stay to watch your back, and that's what I'm doing."

The sisters shared the only bedroom in the tiny flat. At one point they'd painted the walls lavender and changed the old brown curtains for cream ones. The carpet was still the brown and orange swirling-vomit pattern it had been when Keir bought the building. It had never occurred to him to change it, and the sisters had never asked him to. Now, looking at the hideous thing, he wondered exactly how old it was and how many generations of dust were firmly embedded in its pile. He hoped like hell Mairi didn't walk around in her bare feet on that health hazard, and he made a mental note to get new carpet for the rental.

"Agnes isn't here," Mairi snapped. "She won't know either way if you stay or not. Why don't you do us both a favor and go home?"

"Because," Keir said, "Agnes was right. Somebody needs to watch over you. There are more than twenty men out there, all fixated on you. You can't stay here alone."

"They aren't fixated on me." She stomped to the window, threw back the curtain, and opened it wide. Music poured in. "You hear that? They're on the second verse of 'Star Trekkin'.' They're having a campout. They're probably sitting around their campfire, telling horror stories—like the time they were forced to use Firefox instead of their usual web browser, or the day Apple was late releasing a new product. They don't care about me. I'm perfectly safe here alone."

"You aren't safe. You're delusional. And I'm fed up arguing. It's late. I'm tired. I'm going to sleep. Here." He pointed at Agnes' faded pink duvet set, which looked like a holdover from her childhood.

"A gentleman would sleep on the couch."

Keir snorted. "Maybe if he was four feet tall, he would. And we both know I'm no gentleman. Now, if we're done here, I'm going to turn in." He grasped the bottom of his shirt and pulled it over his head.

He heard Mairi's sharp intake of air and glanced over at her. She was gaping at him, but snapped her mouth closed when she realized he was watching.

"What are you doing? Put your shirt back on. Nobody wants to see that." She pointed at his abs. The abs he kept in pristine condition, for the sole purpose of taunting her with them as soon as the sun came out and his shirt came off.

Keir smiled knowingly and folded his arms over his chest, making sure that his triceps bulged nicely, and his abs were tucked in tight. "Are you worried you won't be able to resist me, gorgeous?"

"As if! I'm worried the sight will scar me for life."

"Sure you are." With his eyes still on hers, he flicked open the top button of his jeans.

A gorgeous pink flush swept up her throat to her cheeks, and Keir remembered a time when he'd followed the path of that flush with his lips. Her eyes jumped from his jeans to his face.

"You'd better not be thinking you're sleeping nude."

"Rusty, you know I always sleep nude."

Her eyes narrowed. "Don't call me that. There will be no nudity in this room. If you want to sleep nude, go home and do it there."

"Chicken," he taunted, earning a scowl. "But, just for you, I'll keep my shorts on." He flicked the second button open.

The flush on her face deepened. "Keep your jeans on too."

"No can do." He opened another button. "I can't sleep in my jeans. That kind of constraint could seriously damage my chances of becoming a father. But you can always sleep on the couch if you think sharing a room with me is too much temptation."

"Temptation? To do what? Smother you while you sleep? Aye, that's a serious temptation." She forced a laugh, but it sounded strangled.

"Well." Keir ran his hand over his six-pack, and down to the last button on his well-worn Levi's. "In that case, there's no need for me to sleep in my jeans." He kept his fingers on the button as he toed off his sneakers.

Mairi's eyes were riveted to his hands. It felt like the room was holding its breath.

Keir popped the button, hooked his thumbs into the waist of his jeans and pushed them over his hips. He almost groaned when Mairi pulled her bottom lip into her mouth to nibble at it. Her cheeks had to be burning by now, and her eyes were dark. He kicked the jeans off and snatched them from the floor. It was a dumb move, because all it did was break his spell over Mairi.

She cleared her throat and turned from him. "Make sure

you stay on your side of the room, and don't talk to me." She grabbed something out of the chest of drawers and stormed into the bathroom, slamming the door behind her.

Keir let out a gush of air and ran his fingers through his hair. That was the strongest reaction he'd had from Mairi in years, and it filled him with hope. Maybe, just maybe, there was a chance they could get past their history and find a future together. Because this was it—this was his last stand. If he couldn't get Mairi to give him a second chance, it was pointless hanging around in Arness. She was the reason he'd bought the garage; she was the reason he hung out there waiting for a glimpse of her, like a puppy waiting for its master to come home. He was pathetic, and he knew it. He would have known it even if his brother and cousins didn't remind him every time they saw him.

He sat on the bed and felt it sag in the middle. There were two piles of books on the nightstand between the beds. One was full of hotel management texts, the other had three old travel guides—South America, Asia and Africa. They were dog-eared and filled with markers. On the wall above Mairi's bed was a map of the world. She'd pinned all the places she wanted to visit. Keir's heart hurt at the sight. They'd talked about travelling together, before he'd screwed everything up. Instead of backpacking around Europe, he'd gone to jail, and Mairi hadn't left Scotland.

He rubbed his chest and lay back on the bed. There were damp stains on the ceiling. Something else he had to fix. He did what he could to keep the property up, but Mairi wouldn't let him in the apartment half the time, and the other half he didn't know what needed doing. He should have been more diligent. He should have turned her house into a palace. Maybe then she would have realized he still loved her. He'd never stopped loving her. She was it for him. If he had to give up on her, if he had to move on, he'd just be settling for whomever he married. And wasn't that pathetic for him and his wife? But what choice did he have? If Mairi wouldn't forgive him, he had to let go. No matter how much it ripped him apart to do so.

The bathroom door opened, and Keir's heart seized up. Mairi glared at him before stomping over to the dresser to dump her clothes on top. She'd changed into a pair of black boy shorts and a black vest with the word *Death* written in white across her chest. Her hair was in a messy knot on top of her head, and she wasn't happy.

"I'm going to sleep." She stomped to the light switch. "If you snore, I will kill you." She flicked the light off.

The curtains were thin and the street lights shone through them, filling the room with a dull glow. Keir watched Mairi climb into bed and turn her back to him. Neither one of them relaxed. He didn't know if it was possible.

The silence stretched out heavily between them, and Keir bit back all the things he wanted to say. He knew it was too late for explanations, for excuses. Mairi wouldn't listen, even if he managed to get the words out.

"You ever going to forgive me?" Yeah, it was a dumb thing to ask, but he was feeling desperate and hopeless. This was the longest he'd spent with Mairi since things had gone belly up.

"Probably not, no."

"If I could do it over, I would never have left you that night." He didn't know how many hours he'd wasted thinking about what he could have done, should have done. He'd been in a crappy position—stay with Mairi, and let his little brother go down for his stupid behavior; or look out for his brother and hurt Mairi. He'd chosen the former and paid for it ever since.

"Nobody gets a do-over. We have to live with the decisions we make, no matter how dumb they are."

He didn't need to be a genius to figure out she considered him one of her dumb decisions. "Up until I left, it was the best night of my life. You need to believe that. It was perfection."

The silence stretched out, and Keir thought she'd given up talking to him. "I thought it was as well," she said at last, making his heart clench. "Until you ran out on me. You didn't even hesitate. Your phone went off, and you grabbed your jeans and ran. I was inexperienced and feeling a little insecure, and you ran. Can you imagine how that made me feel?"

"There were reasons—"

"I know, your mates needed you to help boost a car." Sarcasm dripped from her words. "I don't want to hear it. I'm over it. I don't need explanations. I don't want them. I don't want to think about that night. Or you."

Keir scrunched his eyes tight. What a bloody screw-up. There was no end to the fallout from his decision. One minute he'd been in heaven; making love to the woman who owned his heart, ensuring her first time was as special as it could be. The next, he was up before the judge, pleading guilty to stealing a car and recklessly driving it into a shop window. He'd refused to tell them who'd been in the car with him and had been given a year in prison for keeping his mouth shut.

Only, he hadn't been in the car at all. He'd run out on Mairi when his brother had called him in a panic. His brother who was looking at serious jail time if he reoffended. His brother whom Keir always looked out for. So, he'd run to help, and he'd lied. To Mairi, to the police, to the judge. He'd told everyone he'd been the one to steal the car and drive it through the window. It was his first offense and he thought he'd get off with a warning. He'd been wrong. And a year later, he'd gotten out of jail to find Mairi wanted nothing to do with him; he'd lost the most important thing in his life.

The thing he was fighting to get back—Mairi's heart.

There was the hiss and screech of feedback from a speaker outside the window, and then a voice boomed out. "Mairi, my love, this one is for you." Music started, and the guy began singing along to "When a Man Loves a Woman."

Mairi groaned loudly and pulled her pillow over her head. "Oh crap, they've got a karaoke machine."

As Keir listened to the lyrics of the badly sung song, he didn't know whether to laugh or cry—because they were singing his song.

CHAPTER 5

Morning sun streamed through the cheap curtains covering Mairi's bedroom window, and she opened her eyes to find Keir lying on the bed opposite, staring at her.

"Creepy much?" she grumbled.

"Morning, gorgeous," Keir said. "I'll make you coffee in a minute, after I tell you the good news and the bad news. Which do you want first?"

She frowned at him. Why did he have to look so sexy? It was all kinds of wrong. The man didn't have an inch of fat anywhere on his body. She knew this because he stripped off his shirt every chance he got, then flexed those bloody muscles of his in her direction. She wasn't a saint. Her fingers itched to touch, and her lips itched to taste. Don't even get her started on how much she wanted to bite. Her eyes slid down to his tattooed pecs. They were teasing her, daring her to nibble them. Especially the pec with the tattoo he hadn't had when they were together, that tattoo she'd never gotten to taste, and it mocked her with the loss.

Keir McKenzie was pure temptation. That was why she kept him at arm's length and why she should never have allowed him to stay in her home. Because the longer she was around him, the more she let herself forget that he'd ripped out her heart and stomped it into the dirt.

"Tell me the good news." She tore her eyes from his chest. "I already know the bad news—you're still here."

"Ouch." He grinned. "You know, they say antagonism between two people is a sign that one of them wants the other but insists on fighting it." He waggled his eyebrows at her. "You got something you need to share, Rusty?"

"Don't call me Rusty." It was the name he'd given her when they were a couple. It brought back memories of the times he'd teased her with a smile, or when he'd whispered it against her ear while he made her gasp for him. It also reminded her that Rusty was gone. She left the night Keir never came back to her. Now she was just plain Mairi.

"I almost forgot how grumpy you are in the morning." He smiled like it was cute, which made her frown harder. "So," he said, "the good news is I've shut the garage for the day, to dedicate myself to the role of your bodyguard."

Mairi pressed her face into her pillow and groaned. "Why is that the good news?"

"Because the bad news is there's a hot air balloon floating over Arness, with the words *Marry Me, Mairi* painted on it. The balloon's attracted quite a crowd, and we now have people outside the building, sitting in deck chairs and eating picnic food. Looks like they've settled in for the day, which means when you set foot outside, you'll be swamped by people. You need a bodyguard."

"I'm in hell," Mairi said.

"Only if hell is full of daisies," Satan said. "You got another flower delivery. Apparently, someone posted on your Facebook page that daisies were your favorite. I thought it was irises, but what do I know?"

"Nothing. You know nothing. And it isn't *my* Facebook

page. It belongs to the demon who hacked me. Now leave me alone. I'm going back to sleep." She put her head under her pillow and prayed that when she woke, this whole mess would turn out to be another bad dream. Between listening to the men sing awful love songs over a tinny speaker, and the knowledge that Keir was half-naked and within touching distance, it had been a long, long night.

"I need sleep," she wailed.

"You need coffee, then you need to deal with your fan club."

The sheets rustled as he climbed out of bed. She heard two footsteps, and then her bed dipped as he leaned over her. Mairi held her breath, aware of his hands either side of her head and his body caging hers. Even through her duvet, she could feel his warmth along her back. It took all of her self-control, and two fistfuls of sheet, to stop from turning over and pulling him to her.

"I can make this all go away, Rusty," the devil whispered to her. "Just say the word, and we'll ride over to Gretna Green and say our vows. You'll be Mrs. McKenzie by lunchtime."

Her heart thumped so loudly that she was afraid he could hear it. There had been a time when she dreamed of being Mrs. McKenzie. A time when she'd thought her future lay in Keir's hands and that it was secure there. But that was before he'd proven her wrong.

"Go away, or I'll set my fake boyfriends on you." Her voice was muffled through the pillow.

He laughed, deep and low, the sound going straight through her body. "What are they going to do, gorgeous? Attack me with their plastic lightsabers? Bore me to death?" She heard him pull on his jeans and walk away. "You have ten minutes, and then I'm coming back to drag you out of bed."

"Wait a minute? What time is it?" Mairi had a sudden panicked feeling she was meant to be somewhere.

"Eight."

And then it hit her. "Crap. I need to get up. It's chemo day."

The air thickened, and she peeked out from under her pillow to see Keir standing beside her bed, looking scarily intense.

"You're having chemo?" His voice was low and strained, which had the weird effect of melting her heart—a little.

"What? No. Weren't you listening when I told Agnes?" Men! Did any of them pay attention when the topic didn't directly involve them? "Not me. Gladys. It's her last treatment, and I'm going with her to Glasgow. We normally take the bus. Any chance you could give us a lift, seeing as you're hanging around anyway?" She would have smiled and batted her eyelashes to encourage compliance if she'd been more awake, but Keir wouldn't have fallen for it anyway.

He let out a sigh. "You drive me crazy. You know that? What time are we picking this Gladys up?"

"Uh, soonish? The bus for Glasgow leaves at ten. But we don't need to go that early. Can you phone Gladys and tell her to wait for us? And then wake me in an hour?"

The duvet disappeared from her body in a whoosh, leaving her cold.

"Keir!" Mairi tried to burrow under her pillow to escape the chill. "Put the duvet back."

"I don't know who Gladys is to call her, which means you need to get that sexy behind out of bed. I'm making coffee. You're getting up." He stomped out of the room.

When the door shut behind him, Mairi rolled to her back and stared up at the ceiling. He thought her backside was sexy? She smiled, then remembered that she was angry with him and had been for the past six years. The man was messing with her head. Again.

"Why me?" she moaned.

There was no answer.

There was a knock at the interior door, the one leading down to the garage, as Keir made his way through the tiny apartment to the kitchen. He detoured to the door, hoping it wasn't one of the fake boyfriends, because after a sleepless night in the same room as Mairi, he wasn't in the mood to deal with more *Star Wars* trivia. He threw the door open and sagged with relief. It was his brother.

"There's a Wookiee outside," Sean said as he sauntered into the flat, eyeing Keir's bare feet and chest. "And you're nearly naked. Does that mean you've managed to wear the fair Mairi down?"

Keir snorted. "She's driving me nuts."

"She always drives you nuts. That's why you're still hanging around in this one-horse town. You wouldn't know what to do with yourself without Mairi driving you nuts. You're made for each other. You're a pair of drama queens."

Keir filled the coffee pot, leaned back against the counter and folded his arms. "Thanks, your opinion means so little to me."

"Welcome. Is there coffee?"

"You sound like Mairi. I'm making it." He reached for the kettle. "I gather you met the boyfriends?"

"Not so much met as observed them, like I was a scientist studying life on Mars." Sean grinned widely as though the whole thing was entertaining. It wasn't.

Keir glared at him. "This isn't funny. It's annoying."

"It's perfect. It's your chance to show Mairi that you're

better than her other options. Those guys make you look good."

"Are you saying I need all the help I can get?" Keir said, aware of how sadly true that statement was.

"Aye, but chin up, bro—even with your lack of skill, love finds a way."

The bedroom door crashed open as Sean was talking, and Mairi dragged herself into the kitchen. She smacked Sean on the back of his head as she passed. "It's 'life finds a way,' numbskull. Not love. Malcolm would never have said love. He was a scientist." She came to a halt in front of Keir. "Where's my coffee?"

He shook his head at her. She was dressed in jeans and a red tartan lumberjack shirt, and her hair was wild. She looked feral. His woman definitely did *not* do mornings. "It's coming. Try not to go rabid and kill someone while you wait."

She glared at him, obviously deciding that the coffee would brew faster if she tried to kill him with the power of her mind.

Keir let out a sigh and looked over her head to his brother. "Who the hell is Malcolm?"

"*Jurassic Park*," Sean said. "You need to watch something other than football."

"Why are you here, anyway?" Keir asked his younger brother.

"That's what I've been asking you all night," Mairi said. "Is there coffee yet? I'm waiting for coffee. The coffee you promised me. Or is this coffee just another one of your lies? Like 'I'll be right back' before you wander off in the middle of the night and end up in jail."

Sean turned a laugh into a cough that fooled no one. "At least you two are talking about that night. That's progress."

Keir ignored his soon-to-be-deceased brother, reached

behind him, grabbed a mug, filled it with oil-slick coffee and handed it to the beast. She grasped it in both hands and breathed deeply, and her eyes drifted closed. She almost looked as though she were in love. Over coffee. It was yet more evidence of life's many injustices.

"So why are you here?" Keir asked Sean.

"I came to help you set up your website, remember?"

"Uh, no."

Sean shook his head as he pushed past Keir to help himself to coffee. "No appreciation. And when I even brought breakfast with me."

"Breakfast?" Mairi's head lifted as her eyes opened and focused on Sean. "What did you bring?"

"Buns," Sean said, looking a little nervous at the intensity of Mairi's stare.

"Buns?" Mairi looked around the room, as though the buns would present themselves. "What kind? Cream? Jam? What?"

Sean rooted around in his messenger bag—or as Keir liked to call it, his handbag—and came out with a paper bag. He held it out to the beast. "Have at it," he said.

Mairi snatched the bag, turned and headed for the table. Ten seconds later, she was stuck into a cream bun and a mug of coffee—she was in her happy place.

"I don't need a website," Keir said.

This was something he'd told his brother several times. As a recently graduated computer graphic designer, Sean thought everyone needed a website.

"Yes, you do. How else will people know when you're open?"

"They'll phone me."

"Nobody phones anymore."

"Sure they do. They phone me to ask me to fix their cars. Or upgrade their bikes."

Sean stared as though Keir was a puzzle he couldn't quite fathom. "It's like you aren't even in this century."

Mairi held out her mug. "More," she demanded.

Keir grabbed the pot and sauntered over to refill her mug. He'd learned early on when they were dating that there was no dealing with Mairi in the morning. She needed at least two hours to morph into a human being.

"You're getting a website." Sean sat at the tiny table and took a bun. "Now tell me about the guys outside. What's with the Wookiee?"

Keir pointed his mug at Mairi. "He's one of Mairi's boyfriends, and he's shy. Apparently."

"Fake boyfriends," Mairi snapped. "Why won't anyone remember the fake part?"

"Okay." Sean scooted his chair farther away from Mairi. "Which one are you going to marry?"

"None of them," Mairi said at the same time as Keir said, "Me."

Sean's jaw dropped as he looked between the two of them. "You're getting married? To each other?"

"No." Mairi reached for another bun and bit off a chunk, while flashing Keir a defiant glare.

"Yes," Keir said. "It's the only way to make this go away."

"Over my dead body," Mairi muttered through a mouthful of food.

"I don't think that's legal," Keir said. "You know, you could show a little more gratitude. I'm trying to help you here."

"Is that what you're trying to do?" Mairi frowned. "Thanks for clearing that up."

There was a knock at the door.

"I wonder who that could be?" Keir said with heavy sarcasm as he sauntered over to open it.

It wasn't a boyfriend—instead, it was a guy, dressed in a

black suit and white shirt, who looked vaguely familiar. He held a massive bunch of balloons in one hand and a microphone in the other.

"I'm Danny Lowe, Josh McInnes' most famous, and best, tribute act," the guy said. "Someone called Derek hired me to sing Mairi a special song."

He handed the balloons to Keir, who foolishly took them instead of releasing them into the sky. They didn't go through the doorway easily. There was at least five minutes of both men struggling to wedge them into the room, where they bobbed up to cover the ceiling, filling the room with hanging string. Between the flowers everywhere and the balloon-covered ceiling, it looked like Valentine's Day had puked in the Sinclair household.

"Mairi," Danny said, in a suddenly American accent. "This one's from Derek." Then he launched into a pretty good imitation of Josh McInnes' crooning voice as he sang "Fly Me to the Moon."

"See what he did there?" Sean said to Mairi. "Balloons and a song about flying. That's not half bad."

With a groan, Mairi moved her mug out of the way so she could rest her head on the table. There was a strange few minutes where no one knew quite what to do, other than listen to the tribute singer giving it his all at the front door. When he'd finished, Danny reached into his suit jacket and pulled out a piece of paper.

"I need to read this to you." He cleared his throat. "Derek would like the honor of becoming your husband." He looked over at Mairi. "What's your answer? I have a different song to sing depending on whether it's yes or no."

Mairi groaned again, this time louder, and Keir swung the door shut in the guy's face. On the other side of the door, Danny started singing "Heartbreak Hotel."

Keir battled his way through the hanging string, stepping

over vases filled with daises, and made it to the table. "I'm calling Gretna and booking us in. This has to stop. You can hardly move in here."

"No. I'll deal with this. I just need more sleep first." Mairi's eyes were closed.

"He's a good singer," Sean said. "Probably the best fake Josh McInnes money can buy."

Outside the window, a male wailed, "Nooooooo."

"Guess that's Derek," Sean said.

"Kill me now," Mairi said, her eyes still closed.

CHAPTER 6

Gladys turned out to be one of the old folk living at the Campbeltown rest home, where Mairi volunteered two days a week, keeping the old folk occupied and stirring up trouble. When asked about it, she'd told Keir that she was the unofficial entertainment director, and Gladys was her assistant. The tiny woman stood outside the double doors of the nondescript nineties thrown-up building, flanked by two old men. As Keir pulled his SUV up in front of the building, he noticed that someone had taped a new sign over the brass plaque that told everyone the building was Robertson Rest Home. It was now the Robertson Singles Club.

Keir looked over at Mairi, who was waving at Gladys. "Singles club?"

"I wanted to call it the Underground Sex Club, but I was outvoted. Apparently, they can bed-hop like a bunch of randy, immoral teenagers, but they can't tell the world about it. Double standards, if you ask me."

Keir shook his head. It had been years since he'd spent time in Mairi Land, and he'd forgotten that it took some getting used to. As soon as the car stopped on the gravel road, Mairi was out and rushing to Gladys. The old woman was a good head shorter than Mairi, which was saying a lot, because Mairi barely made it over five feet. The two women embraced each other like long-lost friends, and Keir smiled at the sight. This was his Mairi. The reason he couldn't walk away. When she wasn't holding a grudge, or doing something insane, she spread sunshine wherever she went.

"Keir, come and meet Gladys," Mairi called to him as he rounded the car.

He walked over and held out a hand, and Gladys ignored it. Instead, she kicked him in the shin. His jaw dropped as the woman looked up at him.

"That's for running out on our girl," Gladys said. "Been wanting to do that for years."

Mairi beamed at her. "Thanks."

"If I were ten years younger, I'd deck you," the taller of the two old men said.

Keir looked him up and down. He was a matchstick wearing a three-piece beige suit, and this threat was nothing more than wishful thinking.

"It's lads like you give the rest of us a bad name," the other man said.

This one was the same height as Mairi, wore his trousers pulled up to under his nipples, and had a two-hair comb-over.

"Do you tell everybody you meet about the night I ran out on you?" Keir asked the still-beaming Mairi.

She nodded enthusiastically. "Every single person."

Gladys, who wore a purple tweed dress, thick beige stockings and heavy black shoes, reached up and tugged at the curly gray wig on top of her head to straighten it. "The boys want to come too, seeing as it's my last appointment. Is that okay?"

"The boys?" Keir arched an eyebrow at the men.

"That's Albert." Mairi pointed to the tall, stretched one. "And that's Reggie."

Keir looked at the *boys*. "I don't think we'll all fit. It's three hours to Glasgow. That's a long time for three people to be wedged together in the back seat."

"Don't worry," Reggie said. "We're used to snuggling up together." He gave a dirty cackle and shared a look with Albert, while Gladys went red.

"Please tell me they aren't a threesome," Keir whispered to Mairi.

"Sex club," she whispered back. "You thought I was joking. But no. It's all true."

"Best time of my life," Albert said, obviously being the only person over seventy in Scotland with perfect hearing. "No chance of pregnancy, nobody cares about STDs because we're all dying anyway, and little blue pills to help with your performance anxiety—if you know what I mean." He waggled his eyebrows.

"I need to wash my ears out with soap," Keir said.

"If there isn't enough space in back," Mairi said, "one of the boys can ride with my crew." She pointed down the drive.

Sure enough, three cars, two campervans and a scooter were coming up the drive. They parked haphazardly on the grass, and Mairi's fake boyfriends poured out of the vehicles. They looked exactly like what they were: a group of sun-starved geeks out on a field trip—with a Wookiee.

Gladys patted her fake hair and looked up at the new arrivals through her lashes. "You never said we were having male company."

"What the hell am I then?" Albert said. "Chopped liver?"

"They're my fake boyfriends," Mairi said. "I told them we were taking you to Glasgow and I'd be gone all day, so they decided to come along."

"Boyfriends?" Albert elbowed Reggie. "I thought we were being radical sharing Gladys, but there's only two of us."

"Maybe we need another man," Reggie said. "Donald's been desperate to get his hands on her. We should let him audition."

"I am *not* hearing this," Keir said. "It is *not* happening."

"They aren't real boyfriends," Mairi told the old men. "They're fake. Remember I told you about my job and all my online men? Well, this is them."

One of Mairi's guys, the one who'd been dressed as Captain Kirk the day before, came bouncing up to them with a grin on his face. "Why are we at a singles club, Mairi? I thought we were going to Glasgow. You must be assured that I will only be having eyes for you. I do not need any other women. You make my heart complete."

"I think I'm going to vomit," Reggie said.

Keir couldn't agree more.

"Don't worry, Amir," Mairi said. "We've just stopped off to pick up Gladys and her men."

"Men?" Amir looked at the three of them, then smiled at the older woman. "I can see why you are needing two men. You are definitely too much woman for only one."

"Oh." Gladys blushed, patted her wig and smiled at Amir. "I like him, Mairi. He's the one you should marry."

"No!" Keir, Reggie and Albert snapped at the same time.

Mairi shouted at her men, "Who's ready for a fun day out?"

There was a cheer.

"I'd rather spend the day with you, my beautiful Scottish flower," Amir said.

"I know," Mairi said, her grin still in place. Keir wondered if her cheek muscles were beginning to ache yet. "But I thought you might like to experience some of my culture and get to know the place where I live. It would mean a lot to me." She batted her lashes at the watching men, and they crumbled.

As they fell over themselves to tell her how amazing her idea was, Keir rolled his eyes in disgust.

"You're beginning to look good, son," Albert said.

"Tell me about it," Keir replied.

"Okay," Mairi shouted. "We're going to the West End. There's the Botanic Gardens, Byres Road—with all the cafes and shops…" She trailed off and whispered to Gladys, "What else is there?"

"I don't like Glasgow. I don't know," Gladys said.

"The art gallery!" Reggie shouted. "Kelvingrove. Go see some art. And the Transport Museum, it's over the road from the art."

"Good thinking," Mairi said.

"Don't worry," someone called out. "We have Google Maps."

"I've got the Rough Guide." Another voice added.

"We can do some shopping, for our girl." A boyfriend shouted from inside a van.

"Now I think *I'm* going to vomit," Keir said.

"Failing that," Reggie shouted, "you can take a boat down the Clyde. First one who makes it back to their own country wins."

"Reggie!" Mairi and Gladys said in unison.

Keir held out his hand to the guy for a brotherly fist bump.

Reggie stared at it. "What the hell are you doing now?"

Keir folded his arms again and watched Mairi's fan club climb back into their vehicles.

"Should we tell the wee guy riding a hairdryer on wheels that it will never make it to Glasgow?" Albert said as he watched the man climb onto his scooter.

"I think we should let him discover that by himself," Keir said.

"Okay, let's go." Mairi hooked her arm with Gladys'. "Who's riding with the boys?"

Everyone looked at Keir. "No. Just no. It's my car. I'm driving."

Reggie pursed his lips. "It'll be a squeeze, but the three of us will be fine in the back. You're in the middle," he said to Gladys, who giggled.

"Nothing new there." She gave him a wink, and Keir gagged.

The men helped Gladys climb into the back of the SUV before they climbed in on either side of her. Albert said something about killing time in the car with some "necking," which made Gladys giggle again. As soon as he heard those words, Keir adjusted his rearview mirror to make sure he couldn't see anything that went on in the back seat. That was the kind of trauma a person never recovered from.

"I've got special road music for you." Mairi produced her phone and plugged it into his dash.

A few seconds later, the car was filled with the dulcet tones of Val Doonican singing all about 'Delaney's Donkey,' and just like that, Keir was thrown back into easy listening from the fifties. It had not been the high point of popular culture.

"This is payback for walking out that night, isn't it?" Keir said as he pulled out of the rest home carpark.

"Would I do that?" Mairi smiled innocently.

"In a second."

In the back of the car, the trio started to sing along with Val. Behind the SUV, a convoy of mismatched vehicles followed them—with a guy on a scooter bringing up the rear. With a shake of his head, Keir put the car in gear and pointed it toward Glasgow.

"Thanks for taking us," Mairi said, so softly that he wasn't certain he'd heard her. "It's easier on Gladys than going by bus."

"Anytime, Rusty," Keir said, and was surprised when she didn't correct him for using the name from their past.

When he glanced over at her, she was pointedly staring out of the window, and for the first time since they'd climbed out of bed this morning, Keir relaxed.

CHAPTER 7

Mairi settled Gladys in the treatment room on the first floor of the Beatson Cancer Hospital in Glasgow's West End. Gladys was her usual stoic self as she sat back in her chair while the nurse hooked her up to an IV and attached the bag of chemo.

"Last one," Gladys said with a smile.

"We need to have a party," Mairi said. "A no-more-chemo party."

"With those fancy drinks that have umbrellas in them."

"And cake," Reggie said.

"And pies." Albert nodded.

"I'll arrange it." Mairi patted Gladys' hand. "We'll do it in a couple of weeks when you feel better."

Gladys' skin was paper thin, and you could see every vein running under it. For a second, Mairi's throat tightened. She'd started volunteering at the old folks' home because working from home had made her feel lonely, and she'd looked around to see where she could find company. An old folks' home had seemed like a good place to find a captive audience for her sense of humor, and willing partners in any mischief she could come up with; so she'd walked into the home one day and informed them she was their new entertainment director. No one had kicked her out, and two years later, she was still hanging out at the home. The residents had become like family to her. She wasn't sure how she would cope if anything happened to Gladys. Not after losing her sister Isobel to a crazy Scotsman who lived in London. She didn't even have the routine of sending messages to her men all day long to distract her, because some demented hacker was out to get her. Mairi's life was imploding, and Gladys looking weak was one more reminder that things were out of control.

"I'll be fine." Gladys put her hand over Mairi's and squeezed it gently. "You've got a soft heart, lassie. The doctor says the cancer is going away. All that will happen today is what usually happens—I'll feel tired, nauseated and downright grumpy."

"Don't worry about that," Albert said. "We'll look after you."

"I know you will. See, I'm fine here. You're a good girl, Mairi. You deserve every happiness, but you're far too hard on yourself." Gladys cast a glance over to where Keir was talking to the nurse. "One night is such a short amount of time in a lifetime full of nights. Do you really want one bad day to define the rest of your life? I see how you look at each other. Nobody will think badly of you if you give the rascal another chance."

Mairi looked at Keir and felt that same bubbling in the bottom of her stomach she'd felt the moment she'd first laid eyes on him. She remembered it distinctly. She'd been in Campbeltown, going door to door along the high street looking for a job. Fed up, tired and seriously lacking in caffeine, she'd heard the roar of a motorbike as it pulled up outside the tattoo parlor. She'd watched in stunned awe as

Keir parked the bike and climbed off. Her mouth had watered at the sight of him. Even back then he was muscled and inked. There had been a two-day growth of beard covering his jaw, and his chocolate colored hair was mussed from his helmet.

He hadn't noticed Mairi as she stood there gawking at him. She wasn't sure he'd seen anyone. But they saw him. The crowd had parted in front of him, allowing him a clear passage into the tattoo parlor. Mairi had watched him glide through the crowd, distinct from everyone around him. It was as though he was something else entirely. Something different and unique. Something other. Everyone around him seemed to scurry like squirrels, but he moved like a panther. Everything within her was drawn to him, and she knew, deep inside, that she'd found the man she was supposed to find. The one meant just for her.

So, she'd abandoned her job hunt, climbed onto the back of his bike and waited for him to return. It didn't take long, as she suspected that someone inside the tattoo parlor told him there was a crazy woman sitting on his bike.

He'd prowled out, his coffee colored eyes heating with every step he took toward her. When he came to a stop in front of her, he'd brushed her hair from her face, sending electric pulses through her body, and then he'd given her a slow, wicked smile.

"Where are we going, Rusty?" he'd said.

"Wherever you want to take me," she'd answered.

He looked over his shoulder and called toward the people who'd crowded in the shop door to watch them, their faces a mixture of awe and amusement. "Got a spare helmet, Stew?"

A few seconds later, one came flying and Keir snatched it out of the air. He'd put it on Mairi's head and strapped it up slowly, all the while staring into her eyes.

"Budge up," he'd said, and climbed on in front of her. He'd

grabbed her hand and tugged up her against his back. "Hold on tight, Rusty. I'm going to take you for the ride of your life."

Mairi had done exactly what he said, feeling his strength and heat against her as she pressed into him. The world had faded away as the bike roared to life. Not once did Mairi look back. She knew, without a doubt, that she was where she was meant to be. She was with him.

A fragile hand tightened on hers, bringing her back to the present. She blinked away the memories to look into Gladys' understanding eyes.

"I know I should tell you not to let bitterness ruin your life, my girl," Gladys said, "that storing up regrets is harmful to the soul, and maybe you should give the boy a chance to prove he's grown up some since the last time. But I'm going to tell you this instead—take him to bed and have some fun. Worry about the big stuff later."

"Gladys!" Mairi said. "That's terrible advice."

"I know." Gladys smiled. "But look at those muscles. If I were thirty years younger, I'd arm-wrestle you for him."

"And we'd beat him to a pulp," Albert said as he glared over at Keir.

"Don't I know it." Gladys winked at Mairi. "Now go away. Have lunch with your boy there while I spend some time with mine."

"I'll go have lunch, because I'm hungry, but he isn't my boy, Gladys," Mairi said. "He blew that chance years ago."

"Just make sure you aren't cutting off your nose to spite your face, lassie."

"Yeah, right. I'm going to take relationship advice from a woman who can't decide between two men."

Mairi pressed a kiss to Gladys' cheek and wandered over to Keir, who was leaning against the nurses' station counter. By the time she'd reached Keir's side, Reggie and Albert had pulled up chairs on either side of Gladys, and each man took one of her hands. Mairi watched as they made Gladys smile and blush. The affection they held for each other was plain to see.

"Who knew a rest home was such a den of iniquity?" Keir said.

She glanced up to find him watching the three friends, with the same wonder she felt. Gladys wasn't going through chemo alone, and when she got back to the rest home, the men would make sure she felt attractive and wanted, just as they had done throughout her treatment.

"Who knew you could use such big words?" Mairi said.

"Pest." He tugged her wild hair. "Come on, I'll buy you lunch while we wait for the treatment to finish. The nurse said Gladys'll be here another two hours at least, and she's got the *boys* to keep her company." He looked around the waiting room. "Where's the Wookiee?"

Jonas had been too shy to walk around Glasgow in his Wookiee outfit, so the rest of the guys had dropped him off at the hospital with Mairi.

"He went to the children's ward to spend quality time with believers," Mairi said. "His words, not mine. I think he just wanted to cheer the sick kids up. He does that a lot in his home town. They love him at his local hospital."

Keir's eyebrows shot up. "You speak Wookiee?"

Mairi couldn't help but laugh as she held up a piece of paper. "He wrote me a note."

Keir rolled his eyes. "Come on." He put his hands on her shoulders and turned her toward the door. "I'm starving."

His touch burned through her shirt and straight into her skin. Tingles ran up and down her body, demanding that she lean in to his touch. It was exactly the same reaction she'd had the first time he'd touched her—and every time after that. And it was the reason she'd kept her distance from him since he'd moved to Arness. One touch from Keir and her girl parts started screaming for attention. Her girl parts didn't care that Keir had hurt her. All they cared about was getting some action.

The louder her body's demand for more of Keir's touch, the quieter her brain became, until all she could hear was the blood rushing through her veins. His touch was gentle but firm. His hands were big on her shoulders, reminding her of just how it felt to have them on the rest of her. When they'd been together, she'd loved that Keir was so much bigger than her. She liked feeling overwhelmed by his size and yet still feeling protected by it. And now, at a time in her life where everything she'd thought was secure was crumbling, it was tempting to turn into his arms and feel his strength around her.

But she couldn't. She'd learned the hard way that his strength wasn't to be trusted. He wasn't someone she could rely on to be there when she needed him.

With gargantuan effort, Mairi shrugged out from under his hold and strode toward the elevators, already missing the warmth of his touch. "Where are we going?"

"It's a surprise." He followed her into the tiny space, smiling at the two nurses who shifted over to make room for them.

Mairi looked up at him as the lift doors closed. "It isn't Gretna Green, is it? Because I told you, I'm not marrying you."

The nurses choked as they smothered their laughs.

"No," Keir said with long suffering, "it isn't Gretna. It would be a bit hard to get there and back in two hours anyway."

"You haven't booked us a slot at the council registry office, have you?"

"No." He folded his arms. A sure sign he was losing

patience.

"No judge waiting somewhere to tie the knot for us?"

"We're going for lunch. That's it."

"Good." Mairi relaxed back against the wall. "I was worried for a minute."

The female nurse nudged her male colleague before smiling at Keir. "If you're looking for a wife, I'm available."

Now, that was just rude. Mairi might not want Keir, but she was clearly with him, and a woman did *not* horn in on a man if he was with another woman. It was a universal law. Right up there with never using the last of the toilet paper while in the public loo with your girlfriends. Women had to respect each other, and this flirting nurse was flouting the rules.

"Thanks," Keir said with a grin, "but I'm not through trying to convince my girl here that I'm a catch."

"Well"—the blonde gave Mairi a once-over, before dismissing her—"when you are. Call the outpatient department and ask for Debbie."

That was it. The woman deserved to lose her hair. Mairi took a step toward her just as the lift opened. Keir blocked her path and walked her back until she was up against the wall.

"Easy, tiger," he said. "She was joking."

"She was not." Mairi had seen that look before. Other women often underestimated a short ginger woman, which showed a serious lack of commonsense. Because, hello! Red hair. It wasn't there to make her look good. It was a warning to all competition that they would go up in flames if they messed with her. "She was being a bitch."

The doors closed, leaving them alone in the lift.

"You're jealous." The satisfaction in Keir's words made her eyes snap to his face, where a smug smile just begged for someone to wipe it right off him.

"I am not." She glared at him.

"Are too." He stepped in closer until his body was flush against hers.

Mairi felt the air leave her lungs. Her hands flattened on Keir's chest, ready to push him away. Only she didn't. Because as soon as she had all that lovely muscle under her fingertips, the temptation to touch, knead, explore was just too much.

"I am not jealous." The breathy little whisper that used to be her voice stole the steel from her statement.

Keir nuzzled his way from her temple to her ear. "You are definitely jealous," he whispered against her, making her shiver. "I like it."

She sucked in a breath, just as the doors to the elevator opened and people stepped inside. There was giggling, and Keir moved away from her, leaning back against the wall at her side. Mairi tried to catch her breath as she scowled at the staring teenagers, who just giggled more.

"Our floor." Keir's voice had dropped an octave.

He took her hand, pulling her behind him, out of the lift and into the parking garage. It wasn't until they were at his car that she realized she should have tugged her hand free. By then, it was too late.

Keir backed her up against the driver's door, pinning her in place with his hips, and then he cupped her face and his lips descended on hers. There were a million things Mairi should have thought. Top of the list being "get your lips off mine." But as soon as Keir's mouth touched hers, every thought inside Mairi's head vanished and her traitorous body took over.

Nobody on the planet kissed like Keir. It was like coming home and flying free at the same time. His lips were soft and firm, his movements slow and determined. He teased at the seam of her lips with his tongue, and Mairi found herself sighing into him. When he angled her head to take the kiss deeper, she was gone. There was only Keir and the magic he wove around them. Nothing else mattered. Not the past. Not the problems of her present, and not her fears for the future. Nothing mattered but Keir's lips on hers.

Keir's mind was spinning with disbelief. After years, desperate to touch Mairi, he finally had her in his arms—and she was everything he remembered. Nothing tasted like Mairi. She was a combination of fire and spice and sunshine, all rolled into one. As her lips softened beneath his, Keir took the kiss deeper, swiping his tongue over hers and swallowing the moan she made in response. Her body went liquid against his, and he pressed in closer, determined to keep her exactly where he needed her to be.

He couldn't get enough of her. He wanted to be skin to skin, naked on a bed of cool cotton sheets, with hours—no, days—to spend driving her wild. Instead, he had her pressed up against a car in an underground parking garage. It wasn't the most romantic location, but Keir still felt like he'd scored the winning goal in a World Cup final for Scotland against England.

He slid a hand over her shoulder and down to her hip, where he held her fast and tight against him, luxuriating in the sensation of her soft curves molded to his hard muscle. Her full breasts flattened against his chest, their nipples firm. Keir remembered well how sensitive Mairi's breasts were and how much he'd enjoyed caressing them. With a desperate moan, he deepened the kiss, their tongues tangling and caressing in a sensual duel.

He was lost in Mairi. The world outside of her had ceased to exist. Which was why the roar didn't register until it was too late. A large hand clasped Keir's arm, and he was thrown halfway across the parking garage. He landed with a thud on the concrete floor, just in time to see the Wookiee wrap an arm around Mairi's waist and lift her from the ground.

"Let go of me, Jonas!" Mairi tugged at the big, hairy arm.

The Wookiee bellowed and strode back toward the elevators, carrying Mairi under his arm as though she were a rugby ball.

"Put me down this instant," she yelled. "I was in the middle of something. You can't just pick a person up and walk off with them."

The Wookiee let out a stream of irritated warbling, which had Mairi rolling her eyes. Keir was on his feet and running after them as the lift doors opened. A family of four stared open-mouthed as the Wookiee ducked his head and entered the lift. Mairi folded her arms, still suspended in his hold, and glared up at him.

"I am not happy with you, Jonas. This isn't how a Wookiee would behave."

The two young kids were awestruck, and one of them reached out to pat the Wookiee.

"You're letting the whole *Star Wars* franchise down," Mairi snapped as the doors closed.

"Let go of her," Keir shouted, just as he screeched to a halt in front of the closing doors. He was too late, and the lift went up without him.

Before he headed for the stairs, Keir thumped the metal doors repeatedly with his fists. He was going to kill that damn Wookiee. The overgrown ball of hair had ruined one of the best moments in Keir's life. Yeah, he was going to skin the big bastard and turn him into a damn rug for the living room floor. Then Keir would wipe his feet on him, every bloody day.

CHAPTER 8

Even hours later, Mairi still wasn't sure if she was pleased Jonas had interrupted her moment of weakness with Keir, or mad as hell. Her girl parts were definitely mad, but her brain was thankful. It had been a close call. Ten more seconds and she would have climbed on top of him and bonked his brains out on the hood of his car—in the parking garage of a hospital.

"I'm really annoyed with you," Mairi told Jonas, who made a mournful noise that she assumed was an apology. "I don't care if you're sorry. You were bad. Very bad."

She sounded like she was talking to a five-year-old. Give her another couple of minutes and she'd make him sit in the naughty corner. This was what her fake boyfriends did to her —they turned her into a school teacher surrounded by problem children. It was one of the many reasons why they should have remained online, where they belonged.

"He said he was only saving you from yourself," Sebastian translated for his friend. "I agree. You can't afford to be swayed by the mechanic's muscles and tattoos. There's more to a relationship than a six-pack." He patted his slightly rounded stomach, which was covered by a t-shirt with a Stormtrooper and the words *Underneath, We're All Different* on it.

Mairi cocked an eyebrow at him. "Really?"

Sebastian flushed. "I could have a six-pack, but I choose to spend my time exercising my brain, not my body. Good looks fade, but intelligence lasts forever."

"I feel like I'm in an episode of *The Big Bang Theory* and I'm Penny," Mairi said.

That set the guys off into an enthusiastic debate about whether Sheldon suffered from Asperger's. It wasn't anything she hadn't heard before; they spent a lot of time analyzing the cast on that show.

They were in the Highland Pub in Campbeltown. Mainly because Mairi couldn't take another evening under siege in her tiny apartment, so had invited the men to the pub after they'd dropped Gladys back at the home. Thankfully, it was a Tuesday night, so it was quiet. There were only one or two regulars in the pub to stare at the group in bewilderment.

The boys had pulled several tables together in a long line under the large wall-mounted TV. Most of them were wearing jeans and t-shirts emblazoned with geek slogans. One of the twins, Damien, was wearing a suit—because it was a night out, and when you went out, you wore a suit. She'd just patted his head and moved on. Then there was the Wookiee.

She glared at him, and he warbled again.

"You know," Sebastian said, "if you're kissing people to see if you have chemistry with them, you should keep it fair and kiss each of us."

It was as though someone had put the pub on mute. All eyes shot to her.

"Do I look like something you can try before you buy?" She stood and slapped the table. "No. I am not kissing everyone. I'm going to go sit at the bar for a few minutes to give you time to think about the wrongness of that idea." Damn it, she sounded like a kindergarten teacher again.

Past caring, she stomped over to the bar. A glance at the clock told her they'd been inside exactly ten minutes, not even long enough to get in a round of drinks. Time was slowing around the men. If she didn't get rid of them soon, she'd end up trapped in some sort of *Groundhog Day* cycle, where she wasn't allowed to move on until she picked one of them. Or—she eyed their numbers—she could just wait until they all got bored of chasing her. They'd lost a few of the group already, due to discouragement or lack of interest on their part—because her obvious lack of interest was gamely ignored. One of the guys had gotten lost in Glasgow when his scooter couldn't keep up with the pack. Surely, it was just a matter of time before the rest wandered off too. She looked over at them and shook her head. Who was she kidding? The remaining men had settled in for the long haul.

Mairi climbed onto a stool beside the bar, which wasn't easy, because the stools were made for giants, not normal people, like her. No matter how hard people tried, no one could convince Mairi that five foot two was anything but normal, and woe betide anyone who uttered the word "short" in her presence.

"I need a drink," she told Ewan McKenzie, Keir's cousin and owner of the pub. "Something strong."

He slammed a can of 7UP in front of her and cocked an eyebrow.

"Oh, come on." Mairi picked up the can. "You can see what I'm dealing with." She pointed at the guys. Two of them had calculators out, as they figured out how much each person should put in the pot to fairly spread the cost of a night on the town. Their words, not hers, because Campbeltown wasn't actually big enough for anyone to have a whole night on it. They hadn't even ordered a drink yet, and if they kept arguing over how to split their costs, they never would.

"Aye, I was wondering about that." Ewan frowned at the men. "What's going on?"

"I'm on a date."

"With all of them?"

"Welcome to my life. Now, please, give me alcohol."

"You don't get alcohol. Not after the last time. You're lucky I let you back in my pub." Ewan folded his arms and glared at her.

"Don't be such a sissy. People get drunk in here all the time. If you cut everyone off that did, you wouldn't have any business."

"You're the only one that starts a fight every time you get drunk."

"Twice. I did that twice. And to be fair, it wasn't really me. It was Agnes."

He snorted. "It was both of you."

"Well, Joanne Granger shouldn't have called Isobel a whore."

"I agree, but you shouldn't have jumped on her back and tried to pull out her hair, either. You can't argue your way out of this. You're on soft drinks or nothing at all. Be grateful I let you in the door. Other pub owners wouldn't have."

She popped the tab on the can and gulped the 7UP while she gave him the death stare. He didn't even flinch, which made Mairi think she might be losing her touch.

Arguing broke out behind her, and she looked over to see that one of the men had produced a whiteboard marker and was using the window to explain how to divide up the cost of their evening. Mairi groaned.

"You going to deal with that?" Ewan said.

With deep reluctance, Mairi climbed—okay, possibly fell—off the stool and dragged herself over to the men. She put her fingers in her mouth and whistled. There was instant silence.

"Enough! Order drinks now. Divide the total bill at the end of the night. That's the way other people do it. That's the way you're doing it. Sebastian, take their drink orders and come to the bar." Amir opened his mouth to say something, and Mairi held up her hand. "Don't. Not another word. Just order."

She stalked over to the bar and climbed back up onto the stool, which took three attempts. When she looked at Ewan, he was suspiciously straight-faced.

"Can I get a snack? Is that allowed?" Mairi asked.

"Sure. As long as it isn't something you can throw."

"I hate McKenzies," Mairi grumbled.

A hand landed on her shoulder, and she knew it was Keir even before she looked up. "Thanks, Rusty, that means the world to us." He sat on the stool beside her.

She glared at him. He didn't have to climb up. No, he just sat, because he had freakishly long legs, which meant the stool was at a convenient bum height.

"Ewan won't let me have alcohol." Mairi had no problem selling Keir's cousin out. "Sort him out, will you?"

"Sure," Keir said with a twinkle in his eye that did strange things to her stomach and made her clench her thighs together. "But I can't take on family for just anyone. I could do it for a wife. A wife would definitely take priority over a cousin. You about ready to make that decision?"

"Wife?" Ewan's eyebrows shot so far up his forehead that they almost made it to his hairline.

Keir gestured at the men. "They're here to marry her. Someone hacked her business page and told her fake boyfriends that she wants a real husband. They don't plan to leave until one of them wins. I volunteered to sacrifice my bachelor status to get her out of this mess. She doesn't appreciate it."

She just growled at him.

Keir grinned at his cousin. "Isn't she cute?"

"Like a kitten," Ewan said.

The kitten was preparing to unleash jaguar-sized claws, when Sebastian elbowed his way between Keir and Mairi, flashing a glare at Keir as he did so.

"I would like to make an order," he said to Ewan, who just stood there, staring at him.

Keir smothered a smile, and Mairi fought the urge to hit her head on the bar.

"Does he speak English?" Sebastian asked her. "Or Gaelic? I can't speak Gaelic, but I'm sure one of the guys does."

"He speaks English. He's just being a moron. Order the drinks." She gave Ewan a pointed look, and his shoulders slumped.

"What will it be?" he said.

Sebastian looked down at the notepad in his hand. "Three Chardonnays, one Sex on the Beach, three cosmopolitans, one piña colada, one Blue Hawaii, three raspberry ciders, three low-alcohol beers, three shandies, four Red Bulls and one Guinness."

When he'd finished giving the order, his eyes remained down, and his cheeks flushed. It took a second for Mairi to realize he was embarrassed by the order he'd given and expected to be ridiculed by Keir and Ewan. Hell no. Not on her watch. She sat up straight, her eyes going from Sebastian to the cousins, who shared a grin. Just seeing that look made her want to hit them.

"Don't you dare say anything," Mairi said. "A person can drink whatever they like. Who decided some drinks were girly and some were manly, anyway? If a person likes how something tastes, then nobody else has the right to comment."

"Whoa." Ewan held up his hands. "I run a bar. I don't give a crap what anyone drinks. And trust me, I've seen it all. The gang leader who'll only drink Earl Grey tea. The knitting club members that order top-shelf whiskey. All I care about is that no one gets too drunk and starts a fight in my pub."

"That was years ago," she snapped. "Forget it already."

"It was nineteen months and two days ago," Ewan said. "It was a Saturday. There was light rain and a northerly wind. You were wearing a fluffy pink jumper." His eyes narrowed. "A publican never forgets."

"Oh, for goodness' sake, get the boys their drinks," Mairi said. "And don't act so self-righteous. I saw you two grinning at Sebastian's order."

"Not the order," Keir said, and grinned at his cousin. "The Wookiee."

"Aye," Ewan said. "We're wondering if he's going to take the mask head off to drink."

"That reminds me," Sebastian said. "I'm going to need an extra straw for the Chardonnay."

The cousins laughed, and Mairi rolled her eyes. "Is there one man left on this planet who isn't an overgrown child?"

The men stared at each other before Sebastian turned to her. "I honestly can't think of one."

"Nope," Keir and Ewan said at the same time.

"Mairi, my Scottish flower," Amir called to her. "Come over here. We want to be talking to you about what you are needing in a husband."

Mairi stood, perching on the rung of her stool, leaned over the bar and grabbed Ewan's wrist. "If you feel anything for me at all, even a hint of friendship, please, turn off the football and put on the Sci-Fi Channel."

Ewan let out a sigh, grabbed the TV remote and changed

the channel. *Doctor Who* filled the large screen, causing a cheer.

"Oh," Sebastian said. "It's the one with van Gogh. This is my favorite." He looked back at Ewan. "I'll be back for the drinks." Then he hurried over to the rest of the guys, who were now in a viewing trance.

"Bless you," Mairi said. "Now give me something to eat. If I can't drink, I need chocolate. Got any chocolate cake?"

"I'll say it again," Ewan said. "This. Is. A. Pub. We have bags of nuts, bags of crisps, and beef jerky. Take your pick."

She looked at Keir, who was clearly amused. "Any chance you'd go to the corner shop and get me some chocolate?"

"No." He leaned into her and put his mouth to her ear. "But I will take you out of here and get you fish and chips on the way home. Maybe even ice-cream for pudding."

Oh, it was so, so tempting. After Jonas the Wookiee had snatched her out of the carpark and ruined their lunch plans, she'd ended up eating a soggy tuna sandwich in the hospital waiting room. It had been hell. Although, without the daisies this time.

"I can't leave the boys," Mairi said on a sigh.

"Rusty, they've forgotten you're here. They're arguing about who was the best Doctor. They've even forgotten they ordered drinks."

Mairi bit her lip as she looked over at them. It *had* been an extremely long day. They'd barely settled Gladys back at the rest home before the boys were harassing her to do something romantic with them. She'd suggested the pub, because it was the least romantic place she could think of, and the boys had been very enthusiastic. Apparently, hanging out in a real Scottish pub was on their list of cultural experiences to be had while wooing her. Keir was right: she had lost their attention to the Doctor.

"Okay," she said. "But I want cake, too."

"You got it, gorgeous. Anything you want."

Mairi wished that were true. Because in that moment, she wanted time to reverse and to find herself back in bed with Keir all those years ago. Only this time, she wouldn't let him leave. This sort of thinking was exactly the reason she'd spent years avoiding him. He was like a tick. He burrowed under your skin and there was no way to get him out. Next thing you knew, you were running a fever and wondering if you were going to survive. She put her hands to her cheeks. Yep. They were flushed. The fever had started already.

"Let's go," she said grumpily as she launched herself off the stool.

This was what her life had come to. She could spend the evening with the only man she'd ever trusted enough to love —only to have him betray that trust—or with a crowd of geeks who lost interest in her as soon as *Doctor Who* appeared. At least Keir promised her cake.

"There had better be chocolate at the end of this ride," she said as she stalked toward the door.

"Don't worry, Rusty, I'll take care of you."

Her stomach somersaulted at his words, but she knew he didn't mean them. Not the way she'd felt them deep inside. In a place that shouldn't be feeling anything for Keir at all.

He put his hand on the small of her back and led her to the exit. His touch seared, and Mairi fought back her reaction. He didn't mean anything by it, and she couldn't afford to lose her mind again, the way she'd done in the parking garage. Kissing him had been a mistake. It had dredged up feelings that were best left buried and opened the door to desires she'd long ago locked up tight. It was best for both of them if it never happened again.

At the door, she glanced back at her men—not one of them had noticed she was leaving.

CHAPTER 9

They ate fish and chips, drenched with salt and vinegar, while sitting on the bench overlooking the bluff. The wind from the Atlantic had a bite to it, which made Keir grateful for the hot food sitting in his lap. He would have been even more grateful if Mairi had been snuggled against his side, but she wasn't. She was as far away from him as she could get without leaving the bench.

Below them, unseen in the darkness, waves battered the craggy coastline, setting up a steady rhythm to fill the silence between them. Silence Keir wasn't sure how to break without pushing Mairi further away. He'd made good progress with her today, gotten further than he'd managed to in years of trying, and he didn't want to go back. She'd stopped telling him not to call her Rusty. She didn't move away from him when he drew near. And best of all, he'd gotten to kiss her. Now, all he wanted was more. If he had his way, he'd have thrown his food to the seagulls, grabbed his woman and carried on where they left off in the hospital parking garage.

"That kiss was a one-off," Mairi broke the silence,

addressing the elephant on the bluff. "I don't want you to think there will be a repeat performance."

And just like that, Keir lost his appetite. He leaned back in the cold wooden seat, knees wide, arm stretched along the back, but still Mairi was out of reach. It seemed that no matter what he did, Mairi was always out of reach. She was also talking rubbish.

"That kiss was phenomenal," he said. "It would be criminal not to repeat it."

"Please. The kiss was average."

She rolled her eyes as the orange glow from the street lights hit her hair and made it look like she had a halo. He snorted at the sight. Mairi was no angel.

"That's why you were clinging to me like a limpet, and mad as hell when the Wookiee snatched you away." And there was a sentence he never thought he'd say. "Because it was *average?*"

"Even if Jonas hadn't acted like a four-year-old retrieving his favorite toy from another kid who'd stolen it, that kiss was coming to an end."

"You were trying to climb me like I was a tree and you were a monkey. I bet, given five more minutes, I could have had you naked in the back of my car." Bloody "average" kiss his backside.

"Look, I realize you think you're God's gift to women, but the truth is, the kiss was average. I know this is a blow to your male ego, but you keep telling me you've grown up these past few years, so suck it up like a man."

"That's it." He crumpled up his fish and chip paper and dumped it on the ground at his feet. "Get over here. I'm going to prove to you that the kiss was way above average."

"What? No!" She jumped to her feet and took two steps back, still clinging to her food. "I told you the kiss was average. Why would I want to repeat it?"

"Because you're lying, Rusty, and one kiss will prove it." Keir got off the bench and stalked toward her. Mairi held out her hands, which were full of the unwrapped newspaper bundle that held her meal.

"Back off," she said. "I'm serious. There will be no more kissing."

Yeah, he might have believed she was serious if her eyes weren't sparkling and she wasn't trying hard not to laugh.

"There will definitely be kissing. A man has a right to clear his name, and you have maligned mine with your accusation that I have an average technique."

"Maligned?" She grinned, then quickly changed it to a frown. "Do you even know what that means?" She took two more steps back.

"I demand a fair trial." Keir sped up, closing the gap between them. "I demand a do-over."

Her eyes were still sparkling, and she was trying not to grin. The sight made Keir's blood heat and convinced him that proving his kissing prowess was the right way to go—for both of them.

"You can't always get what you want, Keir. You'll just have to live with the fact you can't kiss worth a damn."

"We'll see about that." He closed the gap between them in one step and reached for her.

Mairi squealed, and a laugh escaped on the heel of it.

"Not going to happen," she taunted. "I don't want any more of your soggy, average kisses."

"Soggy?" That was it. He lunged for her.

Mairi jerked away from him. Her eyes widened. Her footing slipped. Keir felt time slow as she fell over the edge of the bluff and into the blackness. He threw himself after her, grabbing her shirt to stop her from plummeting. It was too late. She went over the cliff, taking him with her.

Mairi screamed. Her food went flying. She grasped for Keir and held on tight. But it was too late. She was falling. Straight. Over. The. Bluff. They bounced off bushes and dirt, scrambling for a hold to stop their descent. Mairi's hip hit something sharp and then they jerked to a halt. Keir grabbed her shirt and pulled her tight against him.

"Don't bloody move. Not one inch. Do you hear me, Mairi?"

Yes, she heard him. It was the only thing she could hear over the sound of her blood rushing through her veins. It took a second to realize she was flat on her back with Keir on top of her.

"Are we at the bottom?" Somehow she'd thought it would be a longer fall. But, hey, she was alive, and that was good.

"No. We're not at the bottom. We're about halfway down."

He couldn't have said anything worse. Okay, maybe he could have. Something like "you've landed on a spike and you're about to die" would be worse. But halfway? In the dark? The sound of the waves crashing beneath them suddenly became unbearably loud. It even managed to block out the thumping of her heart, for a moment.

By the light of the moon, she could make out Keir's head above her. He was looking around, and he was grim.

"We're on a narrow ledge," Keir said. "It seems stable enough. There's a huge patch of thistles growing out from under the edge. I think they help stabilize this part of the cliff." He looked down at her, his face in shadow. "Can you sit up? Are you hurt? Anything broken?"

"I just fell down a cliff, bumping around while I did it— everything hurts. Plus, I can't breathe. You weigh a ton."

He immediately took more of his weight on his arms. "Anything broken?"

"I don't think so." Did self-esteem count?

"Okay, sit up, but try to move slow and easy. I'm not sure how stable this ledge is."

Mairi pushed at his chest. "Get out of the way."

"I see your usually sunny disposition wasn't harmed, so I guess you didn't bump your head."

"Get out of the way, donkey breath, so I can get up."

He shook his head at the donkey breath comment, but carefully inched off her and to the side. Mairi noticed he'd put himself on the outside of the ledge, protecting her from falling further, and for some reason, that irritated her more. It took a bit of shuffling around, but they both ended up with their backs to the cliff and their knees up in front of them as they looked out over the black water.

"This isn't good," Mairi said.

Keir snorted. "No kidding."

Mairi cautiously checked herself for injuries and was relieved to find it was mostly scrapes and bruises. She was okay about that—what she wasn't okay with was the amount of dirt and plant life in her hair. She frantically finger-combed it, to get out what she could, hoping that she didn't miss something that would burrow deeper and set up a home for itself. This was the problem with having thick, curly hair. Things could go into it and never come out. She'd once lost a pencil in there and only found it after she'd been stabbed in her sleep.

"What are you doing?" Keir snapped. "Sit still. You're shaking the earth loose."

"Don't worry. We can replace it with the dirt in my hair."

She was itchy, imagining all the insects that were now at home on her head. It was just like when she was at school, and they'd send home a notice about lice. Those lice notices were Mairi's greatest fear because if she'd gotten lice, she would never have been rid of them. She would have ended up the bald lice girl of Campbeltown.

"Why the hell are you muttering about lice?" Keir grabbed her hands and held them tight in his. "Do you have concussion? Are you imagining things?"

"No, I'm not imagining things, and my head is fine. Sore, but fine." She was pretty sure there was an egg-sized bump back there, but it could have been the colony home of a million ants who'd moved into her hair. "I think there are bugs in my hair. I can't have bugs in my hair. I'm telling you this now, while I'm still calm, because when it gets worse, there's a good chance I'm going to throw myself over the cliff, so I can wash my hair in the sea."

"Get a grip. It's only bugs. They won't kill you. You can wash your hair once we're out of here."

"Spoken like a man with short hair. You have no comprehension of what I'm dealing with. I have more hair than bloody Rapunzel. You can't get anything out of this hair once it goes in. It's the Bermuda freaking Triangle of hair."

He let out a pained sigh. "I see what's going on. You're freaking out because you fell off the bluff. You're scared, and you've transferred your fear to your hair."

"Who died and made you Dr. Phil?"

He ignored her and carried on in that same annoyingly calm voice. "It's fine. I can cope with you worrying about your hair. What I can't cope with is you bouncing around on the tiny ledge that's keeping us alive. You need to sit still, or I'm going to put you down and sit on you. Are we clear?"

Mairi tried to breathe evenly, aware that she was about ten seconds away from doing a Wile E. Coyote and running in midair before plunging into the sea, all while screaming hysterically and pulling at her hair.

"I'm fine," she said. "I'm okay. You can let go now."

"No chance in hell. I'll keep hold of you until you lose that crazy glint in your eyes."

"You can't possibly see any kind of glint. There's barely enough light to make out shapes."

"I don't need to see it to know it's there."

She let out a strangled little scream of frustration and amended her plans. It would be much better if she didn't launch herself into the sea; instead, she was going to push Keir off the cliff and keep the ledge for herself. Then she'd spend the time while she waited to be rescued, picking things out of her hair in peace.

"Okay," Keir said. "Now that you've calmed down a bit—"

She growled, and he paused.

"That means you're planning to shove me off this ledge, doesn't it?" he said.

Guess he knew her better than she'd thought. She didn't answer him. Anything she said would be a lie anyway, because she was so totally going to get rid of him.

"Rusty, I'm twice your size. If you try to shove me off, you'll hurt yourself. Now, how about you put that evil mind of yours to good use and think about getting us out of here? Do you have your phone? I left mine in the car."

"Phone?" Of course, she had her phone. How could she have forgotten it? She'd spent the past few years of her life on the damn thing, twenty-four-seven. "It's in my back pocket. You need to let go of my hands, so I can get it."

"Maybe I should get it. It's safer."

"Not for you. If you grab my backside in the search for my phone, I'm going to de-ball you before I send you over the edge."

With a chuckle, he released her, and she reached for her phone—only to find it was gone.

"Oh no. I think it fell out when we dropped." She stared over into the blackness. "I loved that phone. It took ages to get it perfect, with all my apps working exactly the way I wanted them." Another awful thought occurred to her. "My best hair photos are on that phone. The ones I show my hairdresser to make sure I get what I want. They're irreplaceable."

"Will you please shut up about your hair? With no phone, we can't call for help."

"Yeah, that's bad too." She sat back against the cliff and stared at the black void in front of her. "What do we do now?"

There were no sounds of life coming from above, only the sound of waves crashing beneath them, which meant the boys were still in Campbeltown, watching the Doctor at the pub.

"Your boyfriends have to come back at some point," Keir said. "We'll call for help when we hear them return."

He didn't sound hopeful at the prospect of her fake boyfriends being able to rescue them, and Mairi had to agree. There was a good chance they'd get out their whiteboard markers and spend days planning the best way to get them back up the cliff. In the meantime, she would starve to death while they discussed the physics of using a rope and a car to haul them out of there.

"I don't even know what time it is without my phone," she said mournfully.

"At least the phone has taken your mind off your hair."

And just like that, she started itching again. "I really hate you right now," she said as she scratched her head.

They sat in silence for a while, before Mairi remembered Keir had fallen over the cliff too. "Are you injured?"

He barked out a laugh. "Thanks for thinking of me, Rusty. I'm fine. Banged up a bit, but fine. Unless you count the heart attack I nearly had when you stepped off the cliff."

"I didn't step. You harassed me over."

"Yeah, right."

There was more silence, and Mairi tugged her red tartan flannel shirt tight around her. The breeze was getting stronger, and the chill was going straight through her bones.

"Come here," Keir said. "We'll share body warmth. If we don't, you might shiver so hard you work your way over the edge."

Against her better judgment, Mairi took her only option for warmth and snuggled under Keir's arm. The man was a furnace, and he smelled divine, all musk and male pheromones. Okay, so she didn't actually know what a male pheromone smelled like, but she was sure she was breathing them in. He stroked her arm, rubbing some warmth into her. Probably more warmth than he intended, because Mairi started to heat up in places that she really didn't need to be that hot.

"You know," Keir said, his voice dropping low and rolling with sex, "we could spend the time we're stuck here solving that kissing debate."

Twin emotions slammed through her—need and fear. Fear won out. "It's not going to happen."

To stop him getting any ideas, Mairi decided to put some distance between them. She got to her feet.

"What are you doing?" he said.

"Looking for some personal space. Don't worry. I won't step off." She took a step to the left and sat back down.

Right on top of a thicket of thistles.

CHAPTER 10

Mairi screamed and shot to her feet. Keir grabbed for her, thinking she was falling again. He clutched her hand and yanked her to him, wrapping his arms around her waist to keep her in place.

"What is it?"

"I sat on thistles!" she wailed. "There are thistles sticking out of my bum! You need to get them out." She dug her fingers into his shoulders until he knew there would be bruising.

"Calm down," Keir snapped as he tightened his arms around her waist. "Are you sure they didn't just jab you?"

He didn't need to see her to know she was glaring at him. "Get the needles out of my backside, Keir."

"It's dark, Mairi. I can barely see you, let alone the prickles. Can't you get them out yourself?"

"I swear, I will kill us both if you don't get the prickles out of my bum."

"I'll have to go by touch."

"I don't care if you pull them out with your teeth, just get it done." Her fingers dug into the soft tissue of his shoulder, making him wince.

"Do you want to ease your hold some?"

"Do you want to drown? Because if you don't get on with it, I'm launching backward and taking you with me."

"Tell me again why I proposed to you." He had to have been insane when it happened.

"I don't know. I don't care." She grabbed his earlobe and yanked it. "Fix this."

"Bloody hell, woman. Calm down."

He ran his hand down the curve of her backside, over the soft jeans that molded to her curves, looking for thistles. It didn't take long to find them. There were several spikes sticking out of her soft, plump flesh. *No, don't think about the flesh. Think about the pain.*

Like that was going to help. He pinched one of the prickles and yanked it out. Mairi squealed and held him tighter.

Keir felt his way, pulling out each sharp prickle when he found it. He smoothed his hands over the curve of her behind. "I think that's all of them. Are there more? Can you feel any more?"

She wiggled her rear against his palms and screeched. "I think some of them snapped off. I'm taking my jeans down. You need to get them out of my bum."

As much as Keir wanted to get Mairi out of her jeans, this wasn't the time or the place. "They can't have snapped off under your jeans. You're imagining it."

"No, I'm imagining throwing you over the edge and listening to the satisfying splash you'll make when you hit the water." She fumbled for her zipper. "Move back. I need space to get these down."

"Mairi, think about this. You're probably just sore from the spikes that were in you. There can't be anything left in there for me to pull out. Or if there is, it will be too small to get without tweezers."

Logic was wasted on her. She struggled against his hold and shoved her jeans and underwear down to her knees.

When she straightened back up, Keir's lips were almost level with paradise. All of the blood that he needed in his brain rushed south, leaving him dizzy, frustrated and very, very horny.

"Get the prickles," Mairi ordered him.

There was nothing to do but sacrifice his good sense to the cause. With smooth, gentle strokes, he traced the curve of Mairi's backside.

"Do you feel anything?" She tightened her hold on his shoulders, and Keir found he was beyond caring that there would be bruises.

Her backside was a thing of fantasy. It was round, full and perfectly heart-shaped. And he had his hands on it.

"Keir." She shook him. "Are you listening to me? Do you feel anything?"

"Perfection," he said. "I feel perfection."

She stilled. "Are you looking for prickles or copping a feel?"

He looked up at her but saw only shadow and an outline of wild, sexy hair. "Mairi, I have my hands on your backside. Of course I'm copping a feel. But I haven't touched any prickles. I think you're just sore from the spikes we got out."

"My backside is going to be covered in red lumps and sore for days. This isn't the first time I've had a run-in with our national flower. It hates me."

"Poor baby." Keir soothed her abused skin.

Mairi relaxed into him. "That feels good." Then she stilled. "Uh, Keir? You want to get your hands off my bum now?"

"Not really." Keir thought it was best to be honest. "But

even I know that getting frisky on this ledge is nothing more than a death wish."

He gave her backside one last squeeze, making her gasp, before he moved his hands to the much safer area of her hips and kept a hand on her while she fastened her jeans. At last, Mairi was ready to sit. Only she didn't.

"My bum hurts. I can't sit on the hard ground."

"Come here." Keir sat back against the cliff, took her hand and pulled her into his lap.

He widened his legs, so she sat with her knees over one of his thighs and part of her backside supported on the other. Under the rest of her sore rear, there was air. "Better?" he said.

"Thanks." She put her head on his shoulder and cuddled into his embrace.

If they hadn't been trapped in such a precarious situation, it would have felt amazing.

"You're hard work," he told her.

"I know. It's one of the reasons I'm never getting married. I'd eventually drive them nuts."

Keir's heart clenched. "Some men like to be driven nuts."

"Yeah, right."

As Keir held Mairi close, he wondered how long it would take before they were rescued. This evening was not going the way Keir had envisioned. He'd hoped for more kissing and that he'd be able to talk Mairi into pushing the twin beds in her bedroom together, so he could hold her while she slept. Hell, he wasn't even talking about sex. He'd just wanted to spend the night with her. Instead, he was precariously perched halfway down a cliff, on a ledge that was barely big enough to hold them both.

Overhead, they heard cars pull up on the grassy embankment and stop. The boyfriends had arrived and would, hopefully, be able to rescue them. Mairi sucked in a deep breath and shouted, but the noise was drowned out by the waves. She tried again, but the same thing happened.

"I'll shout," Keir said.

But before he could make a sound, music blasted out, and then one of the men started singing.

"Oh no," Mairi groaned. "They're going to serenade me while I die."

"Nobody's going to die. We just have to wait for a break in the singing, then we'll both shout." He held her close, enjoying having her in his arms, no matter what had caused her to be there.

"Keir?" Mairi said.

"Mmm?"

"I need to go to the bathroom."

CHAPTER 11

Mairi was sound asleep when someone gently shook her awake. She batted at them to make them go away. It was too light in the room. "Pull the curtains," she said.

"Rusty, wake up. The rescue effort has turned up."

Keir? She buried her nose in his neck and inhaled. Definitely Keir, and this wasn't her bed. She shifted, wincing as pain spiked from her behind. With it came the memory of the night before. And with that came the unwelcome realization that they were still on the cliff.

"I can't believe I fell asleep," she grumbled against his throat.

"I can't believe we didn't fall off the cliff while we were sleeping."

He had a point. She opened her eyes and was instantly blinded by the sun glinting off the water.

"Mairi! Keir!" someone called out above them.

"That's Donna," Mairi said. She'd recognize Donna's voice anywhere. None of her other sisters sounded that hysterical.

"Aye, we're being rescued." Keir brushed the hair back

from her face and looked down at her. "Good morning, gorgeous."

She looked up at him, and it was as though the world just faded away. Her stomach tightened. Her heart ached. She'd missed him so much. When he'd disappeared from her life, it had felt as though a part of her had been ripped away along with him. Even now, after all this time, the wound he'd left behind that night was still raw and open. All she'd managed to do was bandage over it, but nothing had healed. Nothing had changed. Why did she have to let him close to her again? Now she felt as though the bandage had been ripped off and the wound was exposed to the air. And it hurt again. Just when she'd thought the pain was gone for good.

She shook her head and dismissed her thoughts. Mentally rebandaging the wound, so she could pretend again that it wasn't there. "We should call back to her."

He nodded. "You ready? It'll be louder if we both do it together."

"What will we shout?"

He shrugged. "'Help' seems appropriate."

"An oldy but a goody. On three?"

"One, two, three, help!" They roared together, waited a beat and then shouted it again. Repeatedly.

"Mairi!" Donna called, sounding a lot closer now. "How on earth did you get down there?"

Mairi looked up to see her sister peering over the bluff. Along with every one of her fake boyfriends and Sean. Having everyone stare at them made Mairi uncomfortably conscious of the fact she was sitting in Keir's lap. As though Keir knew she was getting ready to bolt, his arms tightened around her.

"We fell," Keir shouted. "Do you think someone could get us out of here?"

"What did he say?" an American boyfriend said. "Did they fall or were they pushed?"

Mairi groaned. If they got started, they could debate this for hours.

"Does it matter?" she shouted. "Somebody get us up from here."

There was scrambling, and some of the faces disappeared. She could hear shouting. It didn't sound organized.

"This is going to take forever," Mairi said. "There isn't a leader among them. I wish Agnes were here. She'd have them organized and us up the cliff by now."

"Mairi," Donna shouted, "are you hurt?"

"We're fine. Nothing broken."

"Get back from the edge, woman," came a deep Scottish voice above them. "Do you want to end up down there with them?"

"What are you doing here?" Donna sounded a little hysterical.

"You called to tell me you weren't coming in to work until you found your sister. Where the hell do you think I'd be?" There was a pause. "You lot, put down the felt-tip pens and get over here."

There was silence, and then a booming "Now!"

"Who's that?" Keir shot Mairi a look.

"Donna's boss."

"Duncan Stewart is here? I thought he was a hermit."

"Recluse. Bad-tempered recluse. But he'll sort them out. Bossy is his middle name."

Mairi tuned out the noise above them and focused on the man sitting under her. "Quite an adventure, eh?"

His lips twitched, and his eyes darkened. "Not the kind we'd planned to have, but not a bad effort."

Mairi felt a pang at the memory of all the plans they'd

made together. Dreams woven late at night as though they'd been telling each other secrets.

"Mairi, you okay?" His voice was gentle and made her feel vulnerable. Something she just couldn't bear.

She squared her shoulders and pretended that those plans had meant nothing to her. "Definitely not as good as the plan to walk the Inca Trail."

"Or as exotic as the plan to ride the Orient Express."

"Or as dangerous as swimming with sharks off the coast of Australia."

"Or as fun as joining a nudist retreat in Alaska."

They grinned at each other, but it felt sad. These were the plans they'd made together, the dreams they'd had as a couple. They were going to travel the world and blog about it, hopefully making enough money from the blog to carry on travelling indefinitely.

"It can still happen," Keir whispered. "We can still do it."

For a moment, a burst of hope seared through her, and then reality hit. How could she rely on him when it was just the two of them in some far-off country? She hadn't been able to rely on him in Scotland, when she was surrounded by family and had people she could fall back on. No, there would be no travelling with Keir.

Gingerly, she climbed off his lap. "I'm not into that anymore," she lied.

"I saw the guidebooks on your nightstand," Keir said.

Mairi focused on the water beneath them. "Thanks for reminding me. They've been sitting there for months, waiting for me to drop them off at the secondhand shop. I really should get that done."

Whatever he was about to say was lost when a red nylon rope with a harness attached, snaked down the cliff and landed beside them. They looked up in time to see one of the twins—Darius, by the looks of his Coldplay t-shirt and faded jeans—come rappelling down to meet them. He walked down the cliff, releasing his rope a bit at a time, as though he'd done the same thing a thousand times. Once beside them, he stopped, his feet still on the cliff, and grinned.

"Pity I'm not in the running for this marriage thing," he said. "Because I've got a feeling a rescue would take me to the top of the list."

"Tell her it was my idea," his twin, Damien, shouted from the top of the bluff.

"You abseil?" Mairi gawked at him.

"Yup, and canoe, ski, play soccer—normal guy stuff. Which I drag my brother along to, because if I didn't, he'd end up a sad geek cliché by the time he turns thirty."

"Tell her I can abseil too," Damien shouted.

Darius cocked an eyebrow and flashed a dazzling grin. "The genius half of this duo can abseil too."

"No kidding. I would never have known." Mairi grinned back, and there was a growling sound behind her.

"Are we getting out of here or what?" Keir said.

Darius looked between them as his eyes twinkled. "Oh, it's like that, is it? Does the *Big Bang* cast up there know about you two?"

"There's nothing to know," Mairi snapped at the same time as Keir said, "Feel free to spread the word."

"There is no word." Mairi smacked him on the stomach and then grabbed his shirt, just in case the blow accidentally pushed him over the edge. She let go of him hastily, not wanting him to see what she'd done. From the look in his eye, she was a second too late, which made her exceedingly irritated. "Tell me how to get into this thing," she said as she reached for the harness.

It was way past time to get out of there and away from the overwhelming scent of testosterone. Plus, she really needed to put some cream on her stings.

"I saved her," Damien shouted above them.

"You did not, your brother saved her," Sebastian shouted. "So it doesn't count. Does it, Mairi?"

"I'm still down here," she shouted back. "Nobody's saved me yet."

"Give me that rope. I'll haul her up," Sebastian said.

Mairi groaned. "They're going to get me killed."

"Whoever is holding the rope when I get up there is going to feel my fist," Keir shouted.

There was silence, then Donna's face appeared over the edge. "It's okay to come up now. Duncan's going to pull you up. He says he's happy to fight you. Just name your time."

Keir looked at Mairi for an explanation.

"He has a lot of pent-up anger," she said with a shrug. Then Keir and Darius strapped her into the harness and she let Donna's boss pull her up to the top of the cliff. Where a crowd of men looked at her like she was part of the second coming.

"I can't believe you were down there all night," Sebastian said. "We didn't hear a thing."

"This is true, beautiful Mairi," Amir said. "We would never have left you down there if we had known you were there."

"Well, you might have known I was there if you lot hadn't been singing love songs all night long." She took off the harness and tossed it back over the cliff for Keir.

It was strange. Part of her wanted to peer over the edge and make sure he was safe coming up the cliff. Another part of her was second-guessing sending the harness down to him. Because, honestly, would it really hurt him to spend a couple of days down there?

"It was my idea to use the rappelling equipment to get you," Damien said.

"Thanks," Mairi said.

"I can rappel too," Damien added.

"So I heard." Mairi glanced at her sister, to see Donna was standing with her hand over her mouth, trying not to laugh.

"I also ski, play soccer, canoe and lift weights," Damien said. "I not only have a brain, but I also have abs. Look." He untucked his check shirt from his jeans and lifted it up.

Mairi and Donna gasped. Holy hell, the boy had abs.

"Those cannot be real," Amir said, and poked Damien in the stomach.

"Can I check too?" Mairi asked as she reached for Damien. The boy had an eight-pack. She didn't even know that was a real thing.

"No!" An arm wrapped around her waist and hauled her back into a large, grumpy body. "No touching."

She looked over her shoulder to see Keir glaring at the rest of the men. She wasn't sure whether to be happy he'd made it up the cliff, or sad that he'd done it before she got her hands on Damien's abs.

Damien. The twin. She swung her head around to look for his brother. Darius was winding up the harness.

"Hoi, Darius," Mairi shouted. "Do you have abs too?"

With an evil grin, mostly at Keir, Darius sauntered over to them. He lifted his t-shirt and stood beside his brother. Mairi felt faint. His were even better defined than Damien's.

"Let me down," Mairi said.

"Not happening." Keir swung her around and headed through the makeshift campground toward Arness' main street and her apartment.

"I'll check for you," Donna called. "It's important that we make sure these boys are identical."

"No!" Duncan shouted, and Mairi watched him take Donna's hand and march her to his car. "You need to get to work," he said as he stuffed her into the passenger seat.

Mairi slumped in Keir's arms. "You ruined my chance to get my hands on twins."

"You say that like I should feel bad. Well, newsflash, Rusty, I really don't."

With that, he strode past his apprentice working on a car in the garage and kicked open the door that led up to her apartment. All the while, Mairi's eyes stayed on the twins as she wondered exactly how identical the men were.

CHAPTER 12

Half an hour later, Keir stomped back down the stairs to his garage. Mairi had locked herself in the bathroom with a pile of sandwiches and half a dozen magazines and told him she wasn't coming out until she'd used all the hot water, and she was sure her hair was bug-free.

Since she was out of his reach, Keir made sure the doors and windows were locked, and then retreated to regroup. He needed a better plan of attack. The one he was using wasn't working fast enough—not if she was itching to get her hands on the twins' abs. He lifted his shirt and looked down. His abs were way better than theirs, and she was welcome to put her hands on them anytime.

"Not sure acting all caveman was the way to win her over," Sean said from the desk, where he was setting up the website Keir didn't want.

"What was I supposed to do? Let her fondle the twins? Not on your life." He opened the tiny fridge in his even tinier office and took out two cans of Scotland's other national drink, Barr's Irn-Bru. He threw one at his brother, who snatched it out of the air with a thanks. "These guys have no self-respect. They camp out here, mooning over Mairi, flashing their abs to tempt her. It's time they went home."

Sean took a long drink before wiping his mouth on the back of his hand. "Aye, how dare they? Don't they realize they're homing in on the woman you've been stalking for years? How many times have you flashed your abs at her, again?"

Keir narrowed his eyes at his brother and wondered if hitting him would help relieve some tension. "Not stalking. Staying close to and looking out for her. There's a difference."

"Aye, sure there is." Sean sat back in the rickety office chair and gave Keir a considering look. "And it just gets hot in the garage. That's why your top comes off at the drop of a hat."

Keir answered with a hand gesture. He didn't have time to deal with his brother. Not when there was a gang of geeks outside trying to tempt Mairi away from him. A little voice asked him if they could really tempt her away if he didn't have her to begin with. That little voice was just someone else Keir needed to punch.

"Can you keep an eye on her while I go home, shower and pick up some stuff?" he asked Sean.

"Sure. This will take a while anyway."

"I told you already," Keir said. "You don't need to do this. I don't need a website."

"And I already told you that you do. Whether you like it or not, old man, I'm dragging you and your business into this century."

"Fine, knock yourself out, but don't blame me when none of my customers use the damn thing." He tossed his crumpled can into the trash. "I need to get cleaned up. I'll be back soon."

"Keir?" Sean said, stopping him on his way out. "Are you

sure about this? About Mairi? You've been here for two years and she hasn't given you the time of day. You're no closer to winning her back than you were when you bought this place."

Keir ran a hand through his hair. Sean wasn't wrong. Keir had foolishly thought that he'd buy the business and worm his way back into Mairi's good graces. All he'd really managed to do was irritate her further.

"You don't know everything that happened with me and Mairi. She has a right to hold a grudge," Keir said, staring at the wall, but not seeing the shelves, instead seeing the past. The look on Mairi's face the one and only time they'd made love. The vulnerability in her eyes when he'd left straight afterward.

"It's been years," Sean said softly. "She didn't come see you the year you were in prison. Then you spent more years working, building up your business and seeing other women. Then one day, out of the blue, you decide you want another chance with Mairi and buy this place. I hate to say it, you know I'm behind you one hundred percent, but maybe you missed your chance. Maybe the time you had with Mairi is gone for good. Maybe it's time to move on."

Keir leaned back against the vintage muscle car they were restoring for a customer in Glasgow. Suddenly, the situation with Mairi felt heavy, as though it were a weight he would never get out from under. Could a person attain forgiveness? Was there really such a thing as a second chance? Did he deserve one? Hell, did anyone? All he knew was that he needed one, and he needed it badly.

"We were together months before we slept with each other," Keir said to his brother. It felt as though the words had to come out. That he had to tell someone before the weight squashed him flat. "I wanted her to know I loved her before I took her to bed. I wanted her to know she was different from other girls. Because she was. She is." He let out a long, heavy breath. "After Mairi, I tried dating other women. I tried moving on. But every one of them was measured against her and found wanting. It got to the point where I had a choice: either settle for second best and always pine for the woman who got away or throw everything into trying to get her back. I chose the latter option, because settling for someone other than Mairi wasn't fair to me or to the woman who got stuck with me."

"I get that, I really do," Sean said. "But it's been two years. How long do you keep on trying? The rest of your life?"

Keir looked at his younger brother and saw such genuine concern on his face that it reminded Keir just how much he loved the annoying wee fart. Sean had been a surprise baby when his parents had thought Keir was enough, which meant there were six years between the brothers. The night Sean had gotten into trouble and messed up both their lives, he'd been just nineteen years old—one year younger than Mairi at the time. Keir had been twenty-five, older, wiser, smarter— or so he'd thought. All he'd known for sure at the time was that he had to step in and give his baby brother the chance to turn his life off a rotten path. And he had.

Keir couldn't be prouder of him. They'd spent years working through the guilt Sean felt over ruining Keir's life. The truth was that Keir didn't regret stepping in to save his brother, and he knew if the situation were reversed, his brother would have done the same. So, no, he never blamed Sean, and he made sure Sean got over blaming himself. The only thing Keir wished had been different was that the car theft had happened on another night. One where he hadn't managed to get Mairi into bed for the first time. That was his only regret—timing. Maybe if the timing had been better, she would have listened to his explanation and would have stood by him. Maybe.

"This is my last stand, Sean. I hear what you're saying, and it's nothing I haven't thought myself. So, this is it. If I can't break through now, I'm walking away." And he knew it would kill him to do so.

"I don't get it," Sean said. "I love Mairi, I do, but why her? She's grumpy and stubborn, unforgiving and annoying. Okay, she's gorgeous, but seriously, there are plenty of women out there just as good looking. So why Mairi?"

Keir closed his eyes and smiled. Visions of Mairi from their short relationship assaulted him. She was all the things his brother said she was, but she was also much more. She was kind and funny. Eccentric and smart. She saw the world differently from anyone he'd ever known, and she was fiercely loyal to the people she felt she could trust. He'd broken that trust at a time when she was at her most vulnerable, but he'd had it for a short while and it had felt like he was basking in continuous sunshine. And then there was touching Mairi. Nothing felt like touching Mairi. It was as though their bodies were completely in tune with each other. The smallest touch sent off shock waves—something that, thankfully, hadn't changed in their years apart. When he'd kissed her at the hospital, the whole world had ignited.

"She makes me feel completely alive," Keir said softly, his eyes still closed, his mind on the memories of Mairi laughing and leading him astray with her wild plans. He opened his eyes to look at his brother. "She makes me feel like I can do anything when I'm with her. She makes me feel steady. Complete." He shook his head. "I can't explain it. But when I'm with her, I feel like I'm looking at my purpose. I feel like I was born to love Mairi. And that's why it hurts so bloody much that I can't do what I'm meant to do."

There was a long silence, each brother lost in his own thoughts.

"Then," Sean said at last, "we make this last stand count.

We give it our all. I have your back, Keir. Together, we'll bring your girl around."

"I know you do," Keir said, believing every word.

With a nod to his brother, he headed out to retrieve his car from where he'd parked it on the bluff the night before. Mairi's men had gathered together in the middle of their camping area. Someone had made a McDonald's run, and they ate while they discussed ways to woo Mairi that ranged from setting up extravagant dates to buying her expensive gifts.

Keir ran a hand over his hair as he passed them. How was he supposed to compete with that? It wasn't that he couldn't afford to shower her with gifts; he made a good living and had decent savings. But he had nothing like the amounts some of these guys were talking about. On top of that, how was he supposed to stand out in a crowd that was throwing every romantic gesture on the planet at Mairi? If he gave her flowers, he was just another guy standing in line to give her flowers. It was the same story for evenings out, dinner dates, gifts. No matter what he did, he'd end up one of the crowd.

And that was the last place he wanted to be.

At least *he* was the one inside Mairi's apartment, while they were camped outside. It was an advantage he had to make the most of, which meant stepping up his game. But how? He almost tripped over his feet when the answer came to him. The fake boyfriends were trying to *romance* Mairi—therefore, what Keir needed to do was *seduce* her. Yeah, that was exactly what he needed to do. He needed to bypass all that flowers and chocolate crap and shoot for the goal. He needed to show Mairi that the chemistry between them was still off the charts and that being with him was something she couldn't live without.

As he drove out of Arness and headed for his house on the outskirts of Campbeltown, he started planning all the ways he could go about seducing Mairi. She wasn't going to know what had hit her until after she was wearing his ring. Stealth. Seduction. That was what she needed. And that was what she was going to get.

Even after two hours of washing and combing her hair, Mairi still wasn't reassured that there wasn't a colony of bugs in there somewhere. She wiped the condensation from the bathroom mirror and examined her body. Some bruises, a few scrapes and angry red dots on her rear from the thistles —it could have been a lot worse. When she remembered the moment she fell over the cliff, her stomach dropped. If it hadn't been for Keir grabbing her and pulling her closer to the cliff, she was sure she would have ended up in the water rather than on that ledge.

There was a thump at her bathroom door, and Mairi grasped her towel around her. "Who's out there?" she snapped. Seriously, if one of her men had broken in, she was going to break them before she threw them out again.

"It's your temporary bodyguard," Sean said through the door. "You weren't answering your phone, so your sister called on Keir's ancient landline."

Mairi threw the door open. "Temporary bodyguard?"

"Keir's gone home to shower, seeing as you were hogging the bathroom. He left me here as your guard dog." He tossed the cordless phone at Mairi. "Got any snacks?" He headed for the kitchen.

Mairi frowned after him as she put the phone to her ear. "Hey," she said.

"You fell down a cliff?" Agnes screeched.

Mairi held the phone away from her ear and took a deep breath.

"Mairi Sinclair, answer me right this minute," Agnes shouted.

Reluctantly, Mairi put the phone back to her ear. "I'm fine. Keir's fine. We're all fine."

She sat on the edge of the bed, still clutching the towel over her chest in case anyone else walked into her home.

"Donna said you spent the night on a tiny wee ledge. You could have fallen into the sea. You could have drowned. Or worse, you could have landed on the rocks and lain there, bloody and dying until finally someone found your shattered corpse."

"Thanks for that visual, Aggie. That makes me feel a whole lot better."

As usual, Agnes ignored the reprimand. "Were you hurt?"

"Cuts, bruises, thistles stuck in my backside. Other than that, I'm fine."

There was a long, worrying pause. "That's it. I'm coming home. I can sit the exams in a few months."

"You will not!" The last thing Mairi needed was Agnes elbowing her way back into the situation and taking over. When she got in one of her I'll-sort-it moods, she tended to trample over everything and everyone to ensure her will was carried out. Mairi had a headache just thinking about it. "These exams are important, and you left Keir to look after me."

"And he isn't. I know this because. You. Fell. Down. A. Cliff."

"Keir grabbed me and pulled me into the cliff. If he hadn't, I'd have hit the water. Trust me. He's watching out for me, whether I want it or not. And in case you were even vaguely interested in what I might want, the answer is I don't want him here."

"I'm coming home," Agnes said, making Mairi wonder if she'd heard anything she'd just said.

"No. I forbid it. Sit the exams and come home when you're done. I'm fine. It's all fine." She stood up, still holding the towel. "If you come home before the week is up, I swear I will make you pay."

"How, exactly? Are you going to cook for a month?"

"No." Mairi narrowed her eyes at the faded Valentine's card Agnes kept pinned behind the photos on her notice-board. It had been written by a local hotel owner's son, whom Agnes had spent a summer with as a teen. The same hotel owner that Agnes had been cultivating for years, hoping to manage his business once her course was finished. "I'll call Old Man Ferguson and tell him that not only did you have an affair with his son years ago, but there was a love child that you put up for adoption. I'll tell him that the only reason you want to work for him is to ruin his business and get revenge on his family for leaving you alone and pregnant as a teen." Damn, that sounded good.

There was an aggravated sigh. "You've been watching daytime soaps again, haven't you? What did I tell you about that? I told you they would rot your brain, and now we have proof, because that was a seriously crap threat. Nobody would believe it."

"Fine, then I'll fill your bed with spiders and worms if you come home early."

"You little witch." Agnes sucked in a deep breath. "I'll stay here, but Keir better make sure you're safe or I'll deal with him myself."

"I'll be sure to let him know. Now go sail through those exams and become a big-time hotel manager."

"I love you, you halfwit."

"Love you too, big brain." Mairi hung up and turned to find Sean standing in her doorway, his arms full of boxes of chocolates.

"They've stopped sending flowers," he said, looking a little bewildered.

Mairi snatched a box from the top of the pile. Thorntons, her favorite. She looked up at Keir's brother. "You want to watch daytime TV and pig out on chocolate?"

"Works for me." He turned and headed back into the living room. "Put on some clothes, though," he called back at her. "If Keir catches me here with you dressed like that, he'll kill me."

"Keir wouldn't care if I was walking around naked when he returned."

There was the sound of unhinged laughter from the living room. Mairi threw on some old sweatpants, which were a fetching shade of puke green, and a pink and white striped tee and went to join Sean on the sofa. She opened the chocolates, put her feet up on the crate that functioned as a coffee table, and pointed the remote at the TV.

"Jeremy Kyle," they both said in delight as the tabloid talk show host appeared on the screen, surrounded by shouting guests.

"Which one is it?" Sean tore into giant box of Roses chocolates.

Mairi hit the button that would give them the show details. *"Your boyfriend killed my hamster."*

With matching grins, Sean and Mairi settled in to watch some train wreck TV.

CHAPTER 13

Keir parked his SUV in front of the garage, right behind the horse-drawn buggy. He closed his eyes for a couple of seconds, then opened them again. Nope, the buggy was still there. A guy in a black top hat was sitting at the reins, and the horses had left their own little presents right outside his door. Next to the buggy stood Amir, dressed head to toe in traditional Pakistani clothes. He had on what looked like beige silk pajama pants under a long beige tunic, with a dark blue jacket on top. The jacket had a high collar and beige embroidered patterns on it. On his feet he wore what looked like beige silk slippers and about a ton of hair gel on his head.

With a sigh, Keir climbed out of his SUV and headed for Amir.

"Nice outfit," he said.

And he wasn't joking—it was nice. Not as good as a decent kilt, but he'd bet Mairi would be impressed. Something he didn't want her to be, which meant he needed to nip this effort in the bud straight away.

Amir ran a hand down his jacket with pride. "This is my

favorite formal kurta pajama suit. The color will be most complementary to Mairi's beautiful hair." He reached into the back of the buggy and pulled out a bag. "Can you give this to Mairi, and tell her I would be most delighted if she would grant me the honor of wearing this on our date tonight?"

Keir peeked in the bag. Bright pink and blue silk peeked back at him.

"It's a Punjabi suit," Amir said. "Pants, tunic and scarf. Comfortable and practical, as well as being most pleasing to the eye."

The guy had gone to a lot of trouble and had clearly spent quite a bit of cash doing it. Keir almost felt bad for raining on his parade. "Did Mairi say she was going on a date with you tonight?"

"I sent her a text, but there has been no reply." Amir looked down at his iPhone. "This is not like Mairi. She is very good at replying to every message in a most timely manner."

Keir didn't bother telling the guy that Mairi's phone was now in the sea, probably on its way to Ireland. "She's had a rough night. I don't think she'll want to go out this evening, but I'll let her know you dropped by."

Amir frowned. "This is my evening." He gestured at the men behind him. "We drew straws. Not literally, we used a program for deciding the order of dates, but the principle is the same. I am to be the first." He straightened his shoulders, which still didn't get him past Keir's jawline. "I have the carriage, the clothes and a basket with the most delicious of Indian food. I would have liked to bring some uniquely Pakistani food, but I have not yet learned how to cook. To be honest, there is very little difference between Indian and Pakistani cuisine. I am sure Mairi will enjoy this. I had it flown down from the best Indian restaurant in Glasgow. I am taking Mairi on a picnic." He went pale and held up a hand. "Nowhere near the cliffs."

"I don't think she's up to a night out," Keir said. In fact, Sean had texted to tell Keir that Mairi had conked out on the sofa in the middle of watching *Ellen*.

Above him, a window opened, and a red head poked out. "What's going on?" Mairi said. "Amir, don't you look handsome?"

The Pakistani man blushed a deep red, and Keir was tempted to pat him on the head like a pet. He stopped short. When had he started thinking about his competition as pets? There was something seriously wrong with this whole situation.

"I am here to be taking you on our date. We each have an evening planned with you, and it is my honor to be the first." Amir gave a courtly little bow.

"I told him you weren't up for it," Keir called up. "You fell off a cliff last night."

She waved a dismissive hand. "That was last night. This is today. And if I'm not mistaken, that's Indian food I smell."

Keir didn't have to see the drool rolling down her chin to know she was salivating. Indian food and Mairi were a match made in heaven.

"It would do me the greatest of honors if you would accompany me on a picnic, my beautiful Scottish flower," Amir said.

"In a buggy," Mairi said with a grin. "I love it. I'll be right down."

"No." Amir pointed at the bag he'd handed to Keir. "I brought you some traditional clothes from Pakistan."

Mairi clapped her hands. "Is it a Punjabi suit?"

Amir laughed and nodded.

"I've always wanted one of those. Keir, stop hanging around and get up here." She slammed the window shut.

Amir beamed at him. "I think I am in with a chance," he said, making Keir want to pat him: very, very hard.

He turned his back on the guy, grabbed his holdall from inside the car, then headed through the garage and up the stairs to Mairi's house.

She was waiting inside the door, her arms outstretched. She wiggled her fingers at him. "Gimme."

He handed over Amir's bag with a grunt of disgust. "What happened to you *not* encouraging these guys?"

"That was before Amir got me a Punjabi suit. I've been wanting one of these for ages." She tipped the bag up and held up a blue tunic embroidered with pink flowers, pink pants and a long blue scarf with more pink flowers. "How cool is this? Be right back." She ran into the bedroom and slammed the door behind her.

"I know you're the eldest," Sean said from the sofa where he was working his way through a box of chocolates. "And you're supposed to know way more than me. But bro, seriously, you need to up your game. There's a short guy out there stealing your girl with Indian takeaway and silk pajamas." He shook his head in disgust.

Keir wasn't sure if the disgust was aimed at him or the situation.

"I am upping my game. I brought supplies."

Sean cocked an eyebrow at him, which made Keir wonder what he'd look like if they were shaved from his forehead. "What'd you bring?"

Keir rooted around in his bag and produced a large comb, conditioning spray and a six-pack of potato scones. His brother stared at the items in Keir's hand, then stared at Keir. His mouth opened and closed several times.

"You have got to be joking," Sean said at last.

"What? Mairi loves fried potato scone sandwiches. This is something none of the guys out there know. It's inside information."

"And the comb?"

"I'm going to use it to seduce her." Keir stuffed everything back into his bag.

Sean ran a hand over his face. "I take it back. You might be older, but you don't have a bloody clue. While Mairi's on her date, I'll get you sorted out. And don't even tell me she isn't going. You couldn't stop her if you tied her to the bed. She's got exotic clothes and a curry to tempt her, there's no way she'll trade that for tatty scones."

He had a point. The bedroom door opened and Mairi bounced out. "What do you think?"

Keir pressed his hand over his heart and staggered a small step back. Something that, thankfully, Mairi didn't notice. She was stunning, and it wasn't just the clothes. She was glowing, absolutely glowing, with joy. And for the first time since Keir hatched the plan to save her by marrying her, he wondered if he was doing the right thing. He wondered if he should step aside and let the boys try to win her. It was obvious from the look on her face, and her delight in the date Amir had planned, that she deserved everything the guys were trying to do for her.

"You look gorgeous," Sean said as he came to stand beside Keir. "Don't even think it," he whispered to Keir as Mairi spun in a circle.

"Think what?" Keir whispered back.

"About giving up," his brother said, and narrowed his eyes.

"Keir?" Mairi said as she came to a stop. There was a touch of vulnerability in her eyes that made him swallow anything negative he might have said.

"You are beautiful."

Her face lit up at his praise. And she *was* beautiful. Her hair was wild and curling around her shoulders. The blue and pink suit brought out her peaches-and-cream complexion and made her eyes appear even bluer. She was stunning.

And she wasn't for him.

He cleared his throat and reached into his back pocket to pull out the phone he'd picked up for her in Campbeltown. "Here. I programmed in all the numbers I could think of, and it's fully charged." He handed it to her. "Call if there's even a hint of trouble, and I'll come get you."

Mairi looked at the phone, then back to Keir. She seemed stunned. "This is the new iPhone."

"You need it for when you get back to work."

She stared at the phone for a minute, and then chewed at her bottom lip as though she was trying to figure out what to say.

There was a knock at the front door and Mairi looked over to it. "That's probably Amir."

"Probably." Keir stepped back.

There was another knock.

"Mairi," Amir called.

Sean shook his head and sauntered over to answer the door. He swung it wide.

"Mairi," Amir said in utter awe, "I have never in my life seen a more beautiful sight." He clasped his hands over his heart and beamed at her. There was nothing hidden, the guy wasn't keeping anything back; he was genuinely pursuing Mairi. And from the smile on her face, he was doing a helluva job of it.

"Where are we going?" Mairi headed for Amir, still clutching the phone Keir had bought for her. "When can we eat?"

Amir laughed. "Soon." He reached for her and stopped midway. "May I take your hand, Mairi?"

"Of course." She held Amir's hand, and they turned to go down the stairs.

"Don't forget," Keir called, "call if you need to."

"I will." Big blue eyes looked back at him, as she walked away with another man.

"Why are you letting her go with him?" Sean asked as they watched them disappear down the stairs.

Keir could hardly answer; his chest was so tight. "Maybe that's what I should have been doing all along." He turned his back on the open door. "I'm going downstairs to work on the Beetle." And then he headed in the opposite direction of the woman he loved.

It was an evening of firsts for Mairi. The first time she'd ridden in a horse-drawn carriage, the first time she'd had Indian food at a picnic and the first time she'd worn something as pretty as the clothes Amir had given her. Her wonderful fake boyfriend had gone out of his way to make the evening special, from choosing some of her favorite foods, to bringing camp chairs and a folding table to ensure they wouldn't have to sit on the ground. It was a wise decision. Curry was the perfect food, but it wasn't exactly picnic fare.

He'd set the table up on a white sandy beach that wasn't far from Arness—but then, they'd ridden a buggy to get there, so they couldn't have gone that far from town. The meal was delicious, the view wonderful and the company delightful. Amir was funny and attentive. He was smart and caring. And even though he was a little dorky with it, he was really quite charming.

So why was she thinking about Keir instead of the man who'd gone to all this trouble to give her a special evening out?

She clutched the phone Keir had thoughtfully bought for her and wondered what he was doing. She wondered if he was pacing the garage, waiting for her to call, and worrying about whether she was safe. Keir always worried about her safety. In fact, she wouldn't put it past him to make Sean access the GPS on her new phone, just so he knew where she was. She chewed at her bottom lip as she looked down at the phone. Maybe she should send him a text, just to let him know everything was fine.

"Mairi, you are not listening to me," Amir gently reprimanded her.

She smiled at him. "I'm sorry, Amir. My mind wandered. Guess I'm more tired than I realized, and my head hurts a little. That's what you get if you spend your night halfway down a cliff instead of tucked up tight in bed."

"Is there something I can get you that will help? I can fetch you some medication."

He moved to stand, and Mairi put her hand over his, stopping him. "Amir—"

"Please." He held up a hand to stop her from saying anything else.

She watched him for a moment, still holding his hand. Eventually, his shoulders slumped, and he gave her a weak smile before sitting back down.

"There is no chemistry between us. Is there, my beautiful Mairi?"

He looked so forlorn at the thought that it was tempting to lie. But she couldn't do it, to either of them. "No, there isn't. That doesn't mean I didn't love everything about this evening, though. It was one of the loveliest I've ever had." She looked down at her suit. "And this suit is the bomb."

He gave her a wan smile. "I should head home to Pakistan."

Her heart clenched for him. "You don't need to go right away. You're having fun with the other guys, making friends, causing trouble. Stick around and relax a little. Who knows, you might have even more fun if you aren't chasing around after me." She patted his hand. "Trust me on this, Amir. I'm no great catch."

"Oh, I don't know." He smiled at her. "You are very hot, and you speak fluent geek. In my world, that makes you the female version of George Clooney."

Mairi laughed and settled back into her chair. "There are other women out there, Amir."

"I know." He looked out over the water. The sun was setting, but they were facing the wrong direction for a spectacular sunset. "My parents tell me this every day." He looked back at her, seeming a little sad and lost. "They have been pressuring me to let them arrange a marriage for me."

"That's normal in your part of the world, right?"

He nodded. "It might sound like the perfect solution. A man like me, who has problems with women, gets his parent to solve the problem for him."

She knew straight away what the catch was. "But who would they choose for you?"

"My parents think in terms of the woman coming from a good family. Personality and interests aren't a factor for them. But, it is selfish to complain about these things. There are many other boyfriends back in Arness who would be most grateful for their parents to find them a match."

"I'm sorry it hasn't worked out between us," Mairi said, and was surprised to find she meant it.

The sparkle returned to Amir's eyes. "Are you sure this chemistry is so very important in a relationship?"

"I'm sure." Mairi grinned at him and pushed back her

chair. "Now, you promised me a walk on the beach before we head back."

"It would be my most great pleasure," Amir said, and in a gallant gesture, offered her his arm.

CHAPTER 14

Keir had his head under the Beetle's bonnet when he heard a voice behind him.

"Want to eat chocolate and watch *Lethal Weapon*?"

Mairi.

He took a second to calm his riotous heart before he came out from under the bonnet. She was sitting on his desk, swinging her feet and still wearing the clothes Amir had brought her.

"Your date's over early." Keir grabbed the rag beside him and wiped his hands.

She shrugged. "It was long enough, and the food was good."

His stomach actually lurched at what he was about to ask. "Is he the one? You planning on marrying Amir?"

"No, but somebody should. He's really pretty adorable."

Yeah, Keir didn't like hearing that one bit. "If he's that *adorable*, how come you aren't jumping on the Amir train?"

"No zing."

Now that warmed his heart and made him perk up. If

there was one thing he and Mairi had in spades, it was zing. "So, *Lethal Weapon*, then? Which number?"

She arched her eyebrow at him. "I can't believe you asked that."

"All of them, then," he said as he sauntered toward her. "I hope you've got plenty of chocolate. It's going to be a long night."

"Have you seen my kitchen? There's only chocolate up there."

Keir didn't say anything, because he had noticed the excessive amount of chocolate that had been delivered. It made his one lonely pack of potato scones look pathetic.

"Come on then, let's go watch Mel Gibson blow stuff up." Before he could second-guess himself, he put a hand on either side of her waist and lifted her from the desk to place her on her feet.

He'd half expected her to complain about him manhandling her and was surprised when she didn't. Instead, she slid past him and headed for the stairway up to her apartment.

"I need to lock up here. I'll be up in a minute," he told her.

"I'll put the kettle on. If you come up before I've changed, make tea." She disappeared up the stairs, leaving Keir to stare after her.

This felt different. It felt...friendly, and it was freaking him out a little. For two years, Mairi had threatened him with everything from calling the police to setting fire to his bike if he came into her home. Now, she was inviting him in to watch movies. And his weak and pathetic heart couldn't help but hope this meant things were changing between them, in a way that wouldn't end when the geek boys left. That maybe, just maybe, he was breaking through the wall she'd built and actually getting to her. It was almost too much to hope.

Keir quickly locked the garage, then washed up in the

small bathroom next to his office. There were oil marks on his jeans, but the navy t-shirt he wore had managed to survive his work unscathed. With one last check to make sure everything was secure, he bounded up the stairs to Mairi's house.

There was no sign of her, but the first *Lethal Weapon* DVD was on the sofa, waiting to be loaded into her ancient player. The rest of the world might have moved on to streaming movies, but money was too tight for the Sinclair sisters to abandon their small collection of movies on disc.

He popped the DVD into the player, got it set up ready to start, then made two huge mugs of hot, milky tea. By the time he was placing them on the crate they used for a coffee table, Mairi had surfaced from her bedroom.

"Thanks," she said as she picked up the mug.

She wore a pair of gray pajama shorts with an oversized sweatshirt that had a faded picture of Snoopy on the front.

"I remember that sweatshirt," Keir said as she curled into the corner of the sofa, tucking her feet beneath her.

They'd bought the sweatshirt together in a backstreet shop in Glasgow one summer's day while they'd been wandering around the city. Mairi had thought the bright pink sweatshirt with the massive Snoopy was *super cool*, so Keir had bought it for her. She'd put it on right there and worn it for the rest of their day together.

"I wear it to bed when it's cold," Mairi said, not looking at him. "It's good for sleeping in."

Keir didn't know what to make of that. He'd thought that everything from their relationship had been thrown out—along with him.

"Grab those Thorntons chocolates, will you?" Mairi pointed to the huge box propped beside the door, and Keir did as she asked.

She opened the box and put it on the middle cushion of

the sofa, so they could share. Or, so it would act as a barrier between them. Keir started the movie, tossed the remote to Mairi—who would have a meltdown if she didn't have control of it—and made himself comfortable on the other end of the sofa.

By the time Danny Glover had said he was "too old for this shit," they'd made a decent dent in the chocolates and relaxed into the couch. Out of the corner of his eye, Keir saw Mairi scratch her head, and he remembered the comb. Without a word, he got up and retrieved it, along with the detangling spray.

"Come here." When he sat back down, he tossed a cushion onto the floor between his feet.

Mairi eyed the cushion, and him, with suspicion. "What are you doing?"

"You're still scratching at your head. Knowing you, you probably still think there are bugs hiding in there. I thought I'd comb it out for you and check it was just as empty as your head."

"Funny. But I don't think that's a good idea." Although, he could tell she was tempted.

"Trust me, this is as much for me as it is for you. Otherwise you'll drive us both nuts scratching all night long, and after last night, I could use a decent sleep."

"You could just go home to your own bed. I'm sure you'd get a decent night's sleep there."

"Just get your backside on the cushion and let me do my job."

"Fine." She shrugged. If she was aiming for the gesture to come across as nonchalant, then she missed by a mile. "This is going to take hours, you know that, right? I have a lot of hair."

"Good thing we've got three more movies to watch, huh?"

Mairi moved the coffee table out of the way and sat on

the floor between Keir's knees. Her back was ramrod straight as she stretched her legs out in front of her.

"Relax," he told her. "Watch the movie while I bug-hunt."

"That isn't funny. There probably are bugs in there."

"If there are, I'll find every one of them, I promise. Now shut up. This is the bit where he jumps off the building. I like this bit."

Mairi sat tense and straight in front of him, while he swept her wealth of hair back toward him. It was tempting to run his hands through the glorious, thick locks, but that wasn't what he was there to do. Instead, he used the comb to section off an area of her hair, then held the end while he spritzed it with the detangling spray.

"What's that?" Mairi clearly wasn't watching the movie, as he'd ordered her to do.

"Detangling spray." One he'd picked especially because it smelled like Mairi. Like summer.

"You don't exactly have a lot of hair, so how come you know about detangling spray?"

"One of the guys in my last job." Keir started to comb out her long, unruly hair. "He was a single parent. Did his girls' hair every morning before school. He used to go on about how fast he could braid, and what products were best to get tangles out. He carried around a selection of hair ties and clips. Said the girls were always losing theirs and he was fed up buying new ones."

"So, just your typical garage talk, then."

"Anyway," he said, ignoring her sarcasm, "you listen to that stuff for long enough, you pick up a tip or two."

"Which I'm benefiting from."

"Which you're benefiting from."

"Did he tell you about wide-tooth combs being good for curly hair, too?"

"No, that was the woman in the shop. Now, do you think

you could shut up and let us watch the movie? I'm multi-tasking here. Doing hair and watching TV. It takes concentration."

With a forced sigh, she went back to watching the screen. Keir worked steadily, section by section, combing through her hair, only stopping to allow Mairi to put on the second movie. As time passed, Mairi stopped sitting stiff as a board and relaxed into the sofa. He inched his knees closer to her, hemming her in. But other than that, all Keir did was what he'd told her he'd do. He combed her hair.

Mairi didn't quite know what to make of Keir's revelation that he'd gone into a shop and asked for the right tools to help comb out her hair—and all because she was paranoid of things getting stuck in there. She was grateful. Genuinely. Even though she'd washed and combed her hair out, she still wasn't certain she'd found everything in there. To have someone else checking through it for her was wonderful.

Even if it was Keir.

Or, maybe, especially because it was Keir.

As she relaxed against the couch, with the sensation of his fingers in her hair and him slowly, and meticulously, combing each section out, Mairi admitted to herself that, sometime in the past couple of days, her feelings toward Keir had thawed. In fact, in one area, they'd heated right up.

She'd always known physical contact with Keir was going to be her downfall. That was why she'd been careful to avoid touching him these past couple of years. Touching Keir was her addiction. And after years of being clean, she'd fallen off the wagon with that one kiss they'd shared. Now all she could think about was getting more. She needed it, like a drug addict needed their next fix. She needed the high of touching him and knew that need would be her downfall, because no matter how hard she fought it, she felt herself weakening toward Keir.

As his hands swept through her hair, stroking her as though she were a cat, Mairi's eyelids became too heavy to keep up. The movie played on, but it was nothing more than white noise as she closed her eyes and concentrated on Keir's touch. Her head fell back to rest on the cushion between his legs as she gave up pretending to watch the movie.

"You falling asleep?" He sounded amused and indulgent, like he couldn't care less if she did.

"No, relaxing. This is nice. Apart from my hairdresser, no one has brushed my hair for me since I was a kid."

Even then, it had depended on her dad's mood as to whether her mum had the time to brush it out or not. There was a reason none of the sisters saw their parents. Their dysfunctional marriage had been hell on them all. When her dad had eventually blown his top completely and kicked Isobel out of the house—pregnant and alone—it had been a watershed moment for the rest of the girls. They knew then that their allegiance wasn't to their parents, but to each other. As each of them hit sixteen, the age they could legally leave home, they'd followed their sister, and together, the three of them had helped Isobel raise Jack. It had been years since Mairi had seen her parents. She had heard, from friends who'd bumped into them, her dad was more than happy to have his wife to himself. Now there was no one else to make demands on the time he believed was rightfully his.

"If you accept my proposal, I'll do this for you every night." Keir's voice was like warm chocolate, soothing her after she'd strayed into the past.

"Sure you would. Because every guy wants to spend an hour a night brushing out his wife's hair." To be honest, his offer was more tempting than she'd ever let on.

"Okay, then how about I do it every time you think there's something lurking in there?"

She laughed, and it pushed away the last of her maudlin thoughts. "That's pretty much every night anyway."

"You're right. It's too much of a sacrifice for the pleasure of being your husband. I guess you'll just have to take on one of the guys outside."

He was playing with her. She smiled at the thought. It had been such a long time since Keir had teased her, and she found she'd missed that too.

"Now, if I really *was* running that fake Facebook page, I'd have posted a list on there, of my requirements for a husband. And on that list would have been nightly hair brushing."

"You have more than one requirement? This I've got to hear." He was grinning. She could hear it.

"Okay, but consider yourself warned. No man could possibly match up to this list."

"I'll keep that in mind."

"Well, apart from the hair brushing, I'd expect my husband to be an expert barista, who knew how to make the perfect coffee every time."

"That's me," Keir said.

If Mairi had the energy to open her eyes, she definitely would have rolled them at him. "My husband would keep the fridge stocked with all my favorite foods," she continued.

"I've already put a pack of potato scones in there."

That opened her eyes. "You did?"

"Breakfast," he said with a wink.

A strange warmth flooded through her, and Mairi closed her eyes again. It took a second to remember she was listing her husband requirements. "He would be willing to pick up and travel somewhere exciting at a moment's notice."

"I thought you didn't want to travel anymore?"

"I lied."

"Fine, well, I can do that too. In fact, I have a backpack in the boot of my car, all ready to go."

She laughed, and it felt good.

"You want me to prove it?"

He took his hands from her hair, and she grasped his knees to stop him from getting up. "Don't you dare stop combing my hair until you've done it all."

He settled back down and carried on where he'd left off. Mairi settled back too, but her hands stayed on his knees; she was loath to break the contact and lose his warmth.

"What else?" he said, his voice a little husky.

"He would never shout at me." Visions of her father berating her mother came to mind.

"I'd never do that," he said solemnly.

Mairi cleared her throat. "And then there's the sex. My husband would make me orgasm at least ten times a day."

"Easy," he said.

That one word sent a flash of heat throughout her body. She blinked hard and willed herself to move on.

"Most importantly, he would never, ever tell me what to do."

It had become difficult to focus on what she was saying. Her thoughts had strayed to other areas. Like how it would feel to run her hands up those thick, muscled thighs of his and feel his strength beneath her fingertips.

"Damn," Keir said softly, but with definite amusement. "I was close. You're right, there is no man out there who'd fit that list."

Mairi forced a sigh. "And this is why I can never get married."

"Now I understand. Thanks for clearing it up." He took his hands from her hair. "Done. You are bug-free."

She looked up at him. "Really?"

"Would I lie about something that important?" He rested his hands on his thighs, inches from hers.

"You didn't find anything at all in there?" Her eyes wandered to his mouth as she waited for the answer. Keir had amazing lips. Soft and firm, with plenty of places to nibble.

"Nothing but hair," he said.

"Okay then." Mairi forced herself to drag her eyes, and her thoughts, away from his lips. Her head was light as she got onto her knees and shuffled around to face him, aware she was still hemmed in between his thighs. She put her hands back on his knees to steady herself—at least, that's what she told herself she was doing. "Thanks."

"Anytime." One low, husky word that went right through her.

His eyes had darkened, and she saw the same out-of-control desire that she felt swirling inside her. Slowly, oh so slowly, he slid his hands down to cover hers, leaning forward as he did so, bringing his mouth to within inches of hers. Mairi's heart thundered in her chest and she bit her lip to stop herself from launching herself at him.

"I need to kiss you," Keir whispered.

It was as though lightning had struck her. A powerful surge of electricity ran through her body, leaving everything in its wake alive and needy.

"Please, don't tell me no." He lowered his head toward hers.

Mairi's fingers tightened on his legs as a little voice in the back of her head asked her what she was doing. "Keir?" she whispered.

The air between them seemed to crackle and dance.

"Say yes," Keir said against her lips.

Mairi stared into his eyes as the well of hunger she'd trapped inside since he'd left, burst free. They'd been building to this place ever since he'd moved back to Arness. She just hadn't seen it until that moment.

"Yes," she whispered.

With a look of pure triumph, Keir closed the distance between them.

CHAPTER 15

Keir felt like he'd been lost in the middle of the Sahara and Mairi was water. He drank her in, letting her fill the dehydrated places inside him. The places that had shriveled without her.

Mairi didn't hesitate; she wrapped her arms around his neck and poured herself into the kiss. It was a desperate, brutal kiss, filled with longing and regret. A kiss to make up for years wasted. A kiss to release all the frustration and need that had been building since everything had gone wrong for them.

And Keir reveled in every second of it.

He slanted his mouth over hers, taking the kiss deeper and swallowing the moan of pure pleasure that erupted from Mairi. He needed to get closer. He needed more of her. Keir clasped his hands on her waist and lifted her, leaning back into the sofa until she straddled him.

As soon as he felt her hot, soft body settle over his aching cock, things turned desperate. Mairi rolled her hips, grinding against his hard cock and moaning her approval. Keir slid his hands under her sweatshirt to caress the curve of her back and was delighted to find she wasn't wearing a bra.

Mairi ripped her lips from his, gasping for air, and lunged for his ear. She nibbled at the lobe, making him crazy when the sound of her panting breath became all that he could hear.

"This is a bad idea," she said as she traced the shell of his ear with the tip of her tongue.

Keir could barely think straight, let alone formulate a response, so it took a little time. "Do you care?"

"Not right now."

Keir said a silent prayer of thanks for Mairi's "act first, questions later" approach to life. For once, it was working with him rather than against him. His hands splayed over the warm, soft skin on her back as Mairi kissed and nibbled her way down his throat.

"You still taste the same," she said as she licked at him like a kitten with a saucer of milk.

She was driving him nuts. He tugged her toward him, lifting his hips to press his aching cock harder against her.

"Yes," she said on a gasp.

"Too many clothes," Keir managed to say.

Mairi sat back, her eyes filled with liquid heat, her cheeks flushed and her full lips swollen. Her fiery hair fell in wild curls around her face and shoulders. She was a goddess. And he was merely a man. Without taking her eyes from his, she whipped off her sweatshirt and tossed it behind her. Full breasts swayed in front of him. Dusky pink nipples, hard and ready for him to touch and taste. She was even curvier than Keir remembered, and he was sure he remembered every single detail of their night together. Her hips were fuller, her breasts larger. She was a woman who enjoyed her curves. A woman who laughed at the stick-insect models. She was perfection.

"Your turn," she said, but she didn't wait for him. Because when his Mairi was set on a course, she wanted to get there as fast as possible, and what little patience she had was thrown out the window.

She grabbed the bottom of his t-shirt and yanked it upward, forcing Keir to move so she could rip it off over his head. It was tossed away like her shirt before it. Keir kept his hands on her hips, waiting to see what she would do next, as her eyes roamed his chest.

"You have a new tattoo." She trailed the swirling red design that covered his left pec. "I noticed it when you were running around half-naked. Is it a prison tat?"

Yeah, there was no way he was letting her mind go there. That topic was sure to make Mairi think about all the reasons she shouldn't be half-naked in his lap.

"No." He hooked a hand on the back of her neck and pulled her to him, taking her mouth like a man who needed it more than he needed air.

All thoughts of the tattoo were forgotten as she melted into his kiss. The tattoo he'd had inked when he'd decided to move back to Arness to try again with Mairi. The tattoo that symbolized Mairi's wild, curling hair as it lay across his chest. Across his heart. Like a mark of ownership. He was hers. He *always* would be hers, whether she accepted him or not.

He felt her soft breasts press against his chest, her hard nipples rubbing against him. His hands curved around her rear, molding and caressing, rubbing her against him until she was panting desperately and forgot to kiss him back.

They needed a bed. Mairi's sofa was far too small to cope with where this was heading. Keir held her tight and stood, supporting her weight as he did so. Mairi instantly wrapped her legs around him and buried her face in his neck. Her hands were everywhere. Tracing his shoulders, his back, his chest. Every touch was a flame licking his skin, making him burn with desperation for more.

With a kick, he opened Mairi's bedroom door and lay her on the tiny single bed, coming down on top of her. They frantically pawed at each other's remaining clothes. Keir pulled her shorts over her hips while Mairi unzipped his jeans and tried to tug them down as Keir kicked off his shoes. With a growl of frustration, Mairi gave up trying to get his jeans off, and instead, she slipped her hand into the front of them, right under his briefs, and wrapped her fist around his shaft.

"Hell." Keir managed to get the word out as his back bowed.

"Not hell, Keir, heaven." She nibbled at his chest.

Keir was trapped in her hold, suspended above her, his weight on his hands to keep from crushing her. A position that gave Mairi free rein to roam. And roam she did. Keri groaned as one hand swept up his chest, while the other started a slow, tight glide on his cock.

"Rusty," he growled. "You keep doing that and we're going to be done a whole lot sooner than you'll like."

"You're going too slow." She bit his nipple, making him groan yet again. She was trying to kill him; it was the only explanation.

"Rusty, gorgeous, kick off your shorts and I promise to speed things up."

She looked up at him with big, teasing eyes. "Promise?"

"I'll promise anything you want as long it will get me out of these jeans and into you."

With a put-upon sigh, Mairi kicked off her shorts, her hand never leaving his aching cock. "I'll just hold on to this while you take off your jeans." She squeezed him tight.

Keir growled at her. "You're playing with fire, Rusty."

"I'm playing with you."

"We'll see about that." With her still holding him, Keir managed to stand and get his jeans and briefs off.

Mairi knelt on the bed before him, her hair wild around her shoulders, her cream-colored skin flushed with patches of pink. Her smile was a dare, and her hand was still firmly locked around his aching flesh.

The sight made his heart beat erratically. "Either do something interesting with it, or let go, so I can."

"And you tell me I have no patience." Slowly, teasingly, she bent over and licked the head of his cock like it was a lollipop.

"Mairi." His hands burrowed into her hair and gripped tight.

"How much do you think you can take before you surrender?" she asked as she looked up at him, her lips still precariously close to his cock.

"I've already reached my limit. I need to be inside you, Rusty."

With her eyes still on his, she licked him again. "Maybe I should tie you to the bed and spend the night driving you insane."

Under her touch, Keir felt his cock pulse and harden to the point of pain. His balls were tight, and he knew that if she kept going, he was going to come before they even got properly started. He tightened his hands in her hair and tugged, in an attempt to get her to release him. She just swallowed the head of his cock and chuckled around it. Keir's back arched, his head fell back and a whole stream of words that didn't make sense flowed from his lips.

"Maybe I've been dealing with your running out on me the wrong way," Mairi said between kissing his desperate flesh. "Maybe I should have taken my revenge by tying you up and teasing you for months without letting you come."

Keir groaned as the images she put in his head made his

blood boil. She was a demon, sent to torment him. And with her hand on his dick and her lips teasing him, there wasn't a whole lot he could do about it. The power was definitely with Mairi. She was in control, and Keir wasn't sure if it was the best thing he'd ever experienced, or if he was going to lose his mind at any second.

"You're killing me here," he said.

"I like the sound of that."

The witch would torment him all night if he didn't stop her. He needed to take back control, somehow. As fast as the thought came to him, it was gone again, because Mairi enclosed him in her mouth and sucked hard. Her hand moved fast and tight on the bottom of his cock, as her tongue worked the top. Keir felt a tingling sensation race up and down his spine. The world was spinning, and the ride was blowing his mind.

"Mairi, you need to stop, I'm going to come." It was a fight to get the words out.

The little devil sucked harder. It was too late. It'd been far too long since he'd touched a woman. And even longer since he'd touched Mairi. Keir just didn't have the self-control to stop himself. Instead, he let his head fall back and groaned as he emptied himself into Mairi's eager mouth.

When he finally came down from the stratosphere, he found his hands still tangled in Mairi's hair and her frowning at his spent dick. She looked up at him with a little pout.

"I didn't think that through properly." She pointed at his hanging dick. "Now what?"

Keir couldn't help but grin at her. "Now I get to torture you while I recover."

She squealed as he lifted her under the arms and tossed her back onto the bed. He fell to his knees on the carpet beside it, grasped her hips and yanked her to the edge of the bed.

"Buckle up, Rusty—this ride is going to be wild."

Mairi's ardor had calmed somewhat, which meant her mind had space to think. For Mairi, thinking was seldom a good thing. And on this occasion, it was no different. Because in the silence inside her head, a little voice began to shout. It reminded her that nothing had changed. That Keir was still the man who'd taken her to bed for the first time, and then left to commit a crime. The man who'd walked out in the middle of the night and never come back; he couldn't come back, because he'd been locked up tight. She knew he hadn't been in any trouble since, and she knew he had a good reputation as someone who worked hard, charged fair rates and never messed anyone around. She knew all these things. But still, there was that voice. The one telling her that if she gave him a second chance, she would be no better than her mother—constantly excusing her father's behavior and going back for more.

With each second that passed without her body ruling her brain, that little voice became louder. Until it reached a point where all she could think was that being with Keir was a terrible mistake. She took a deep breath and readied herself to call a halt to their night. And that was when his mouth descended on her excited girl parts, and the words that had been on the tip of her tongue turned into a moan of pleasure. The voice in her head was suddenly silenced as her girl parts screamed in delight. Instead, the empty space of her mind was filled with bursts of dizzying color as Keir licked and nipped and teased her sensitive clit.

She grasped at his too-short hair, wishing it was longer so that she would have a stronger grip. She needed a stronger grip. She needed something to hold, to ground her, while

Keir made her soar. He pushed her thighs wider and licked up the length of her opening.

"Keir!" Her back arched and she panted.

"Aye, Rusty, it's your Keir."

His tone was deeply possessive, but even that wasn't enough to distract her from the sensation of his tongue flicking her clit. Her muscles tightened. Her mouth fell open. She couldn't see anything but the lights going off in her head. She couldn't feel anything but Keir's masterful touch. She couldn't hear anything but the blood rushing through her veins. She was wound up tight, teetering on the edge of a fall that was going to shatter her into a thousand glorious pieces. There was no controlling it. Her body wasn't her own anymore. It belonged to Keir.

"Give it to me now, Rusty." His voice was a husky breath she felt against her clit.

Obedience was instant. Her whole body spasmed as pure, unadulterated pleasure detonated inside her. It started at her clit and shot out until it hit her fingers and toes, and every inch of her body sang with pleasure.

She felt Keir's hands on her stomach as they slid up to cover her breasts. He squeezed her sensitive mounds, causing an aftershock that had her calling out his name.

"You are so bloody gorgeous."

It was impossible to answer. She was floating in a place she never wanted to leave. Strong hands curved under her knees and tugged her body down the bed until her backside was hanging off it. Mairi struggled to lift her eyelids, which suddenly weighed about ten pounds each. When she got her eyes open, what she saw stole the air from her lungs.

Keir was kneeling between her legs, the head of his cock poised at her entrance. He was hard and ready for her, and just looking at him made her feel desperately empty. His hand fisted his cock and he stroked, once, twice. In his other hand, he held a condom, and as she watched, he slowly rolled it down his length, making Mairi's mouth water at the sight.

"You ready for me, Rusty?"

At the sound of his dark voice, Mairi's gaze jumped to his face, and her heart missed a beat. His eyes were ablaze with desire and possession. But more than that, Mairi saw something she hadn't seen for years. Something that would have terrified her if she hadn't been riding the waves of his attention—she saw love.

"Aye," he said with a slow, wicked smile, "you're ready for me."

As her brain struggled to make sense of what she'd seen, he lined his hard length up with her opening and slowly entered her. Mairi grasped his arms as he held her hips tight, to keep her exactly where he wanted her. The coiled tension in his muscles made her shudder. He was strong, overwhelmingly so, and in that moment, his strength belonged to her. With their eyes locked together, she didn't miss the need, hope and longing she saw in his gaze. It was all there, laid bare for her as he made himself vulnerable. The sight was terrifying, and she almost wanted to stop him before he was fully seated inside of her. This wasn't meant to be about longing. It was only about touch and her need to sate the hunger that consumed her every minute of every day. A need only Keir could satisfy. That was all she wanted. She didn't want his heart. And that was what he was offering her. It was there, in the look in his eyes and in the reverence on his face as he joined them together.

"Too much," she said, meaning everything he was offering her.

"Never."

"Keir?" Fear made her tremble. Not of the act, but of the emotion.

He leaned over her and pressed a gentle kiss to her lips.

There was no pretense that he didn't understand what she was feeling; he just gave her a sad little smile.

"You don't owe me anything, Rusty. Just feel, gorgeous. That's all you need to do." And then he pulled back and plunged back into her, deep and wonderfully hard.

The moment of fear and vulnerability was shattered as Mairi's eyes closed at the sensation of his steel shaft filling her. When she looked back up at him, everything she thought she'd seen in his eyes was gone, and she wondered if she'd imagined it.

Keir smiled wickedly as he slowly withdrew from her body. "Feel free to come at any time," he said with an evil glint in his eye. "Your gorgeous mouth took the edge off for me, and now I can take my time. And I plan to take a very long time, Rusty." With that, he leaned forward and sucked her nipple into his mouth.

Mairi was lost. All she could do was lie there, spinning in a world of pure sensation, while Keir mastered her body. He kept a slow, steady pace inside of her, just enough to keep her on edge, but not enough to send her over, and all the while he tortured her sensitive breasts with his tongue and teeth.

"I'm going to kill you if you don't make me come." The words came out in a husky, panting breath.

Her answer was a wicked chuckle. Mairi fought back the only way she knew how: she clenched the muscles inside of her slick channel. There was a loud groan as Keir's steady rhythm faltered. His head fell forward, and his shoulders clenched. It was a beautiful sight, so Mairi repeated her torture.

Dark, dangerous eyes looked up at her. "You'll pay for that."

"I hope so. You going to speed things up now?"

"Aye." He gripped her hips and plunged deep inside her.

There was no teasing after that. He pummeled into her,

until her mind was nothing but a swirl of color, and her body shuddered with pleasure. A hand slid between their bodies. A thumb strummed her clit. And Mairi was soaring. She heard a long groan of pleasure as Keir followed her into the abyss.

Spent and panting, Mairi held on to Keir as she floated back to earth. His weight was a welcoming blanket, and his heat made her still spasming muscles ease. Liquid bones made movement impossible. All she could do was lie there under Keir, breathing him in and filling herself with his scent.

"Witch," Keir grumbled as he pressed a kiss into the crook of her neck. "You sabotaged my plan."

"Your plan was to drive me insane."

"Aye. It was a good plan."

Mairi smiled up at the ceiling as Keir lifted his body weight onto his straightened arms. How he had the energy to move even that much, she didn't know.

"Next time, I won't let you get the better of me."

Her exhausted girl parts came to life at the threat, and Mairi mentally told them to get a grip. They'd had their fun. Now it was time to let her head take control again. For a second, she thought she heard them whine in complaint.

Keir pressed a dizzying kiss to her lips before he climbed off the bed and headed for the bathroom. As soon as the view of his gorgeous backside disappeared, Mairi fell asleep, with her legs hanging off the bed.

CHAPTER 16

Mairi woke the following morning to the sound of her bedroom door crashing open.

"Keir?" someone shrieked. "You're naked. You're in bed with Mairi. You're both naked. I need to wash my eyes out with soap."

Agnes was home.

The door slammed shut again, but Agnes wasn't finished shouting. "Get your backsides out here. We've got another problem."

Mairi struggled to sit up, but Keir's weight kept her plastered to the bed. They were tangled together in a bed meant for one, and Mairi had somehow ended up under someone who was double her weight. It was a miracle she hadn't suffocated in her sleep.

"Get off me." With a massive shove, she managed to topple his bulk out of the bed, and he landed on the floor with a thump.

"That was uncalled for," he grumbled. "It's nine o'clock. We overslept. Hamish will be wondering where I am."

Mairi wrestled with the sheets that were tangled around

her legs, tying her to the bed. Eventually, she managed to get her feet free and threw them over the edge—only to have them land on Keir's stomach.

"Oomph!" He grabbed her ankles before she could try to find the floor again. "I'll move. I don't want your feet landing on my balls."

"Hurry up about it," Mairi snapped.

Her hair was everywhere, and she fought to get it off her face, out of her mouth and away from her eyes. Why hadn't she tied the unruly mop up before she fell asleep? The answer loomed in front of her, naked and very much aroused.

"Put that away before you take somebody's eye out," she said.

"I don't remember that attitude last night. I remember somebody hanging on to my dick like it was a joystick and I was their favorite game."

He grabbed his jeans and stepped into them as Mairi looked around for something to tie up her hair. There were days when shaving her head seemed like a really good idea, and this was turning into one of them.

"Go make coffee," she told Keir. "I need coffee."

"Get out of there!" Agnes shouted.

"Where's the coffee?" Mairi shouted back.

"You are a Gorgon in the morning." With a shake of his head, Keir shrugged into his t-shirt and walked out of the bedroom with his feet still bare.

"You had sex with my sister." Mairi heard Agnes as soon as Keir left the room.

"It's none of your business," Mairi called out, wishing their apartment wasn't so small that she could hear every damn word her control-freak sister said.

"She had sex with me," Keir said, and Mairi groaned.

"How could you do this now?" Agnes demanded. "When she's under stress and vulnerable?"

"I am not vulnerable," Mairi shouted. "But I am pissed off that there isn't a mug of coffee in my hand."

"You calm her down," Keir said, sounding resigned. "I'll make coffee."

The door opened as Mairi tugged the sheet around her naked body.

"You okay?" Agnes was in dark blue jeans, beige boots, and a red sweater that made her blonde hair glow.

"New jeans?" Mairi said.

"Got them on sale." Agnes turned so Mairi could see the back. "They make my backside look great."

"Definitely worth the money. Do you know where a hair tie is? This mop is driving me nuts."

Agnes picked one up from the dresser and tossed it at Mairi, who tied her hair back in a mess behind her head. At least it wasn't in her mouth anymore.

"Do you plan on answering me?" Agnes did that toe-tapping thing she loved to do. "Are you okay?"

"I have a bad-decision hangover that I don't think will go away with coffee and a fried breakfast." Mairi looked up at her sister. "Is there a hangover cure for stupidity?"

"Coffee's ready," Keir shouted.

"He's still here," Mairi said. "I was hoping he'd just leave."

Agnes gave Mairi a look that made it clear exactly how stupid she thought that comment had been. "Yes, now that he's managed to get you back into bed, after years of trying, he's just going to waltz out of here and get on with his life."

Mairi stared at her sister for a moment as her cotton-wool-filled brain tried to figure out if she was speaking sarcasm. "He isn't going to do that, is he?"

Agnes threw up her hands and stalked out of the room.

"Give her coffee and wake her up before I kill her," she ordered Keir.

A couple of seconds later, he came into the room with a large, steaming mug. He handed it to her, and Mairi clasped it in both hands, not caring if the sheet fell while she was drinking.

He brushed a stray hair behind her ear as he smiled down at her. "You okay?"

Mairi scowled at him. "Why does everybody keep asking me that?"

"I'll take that as a yes," he said dryly.

"I regret last night," she said, laying it on the line for him.

His eyes sparkled. "No, you don't. You regret giving in to what you wanted instead of stubbornly keeping your distance and making us both suffer."

The fact he was right didn't change one thing. "It won't happen again."

"You sure about that?" He was so inflated with arrogance that she wanted to stick a pin in him and watch him pop.

Before she could think of a cutting comeback, Keir put a hand on each side of her face and kissed her. The kiss had magical powers. It completely defused the irritation she felt, and filled the world with rainbows. When he drew away, she followed, but he just chuckled, kissed the tip of her nose and sauntered out of the room, leaving her dazed, needy and aware that all thoughts of never repeating last night had fled from her brain.

She was still staring after him when Aggie's dulcet tones rang through the room. "Get dressed and get out here. We have a situation."

Mairi let out a groan, gulped the coffee and lamented her life. It had been too much to hope that Agnes would get the bus home instead of flying back from Glasgow. At least if she'd come back on the bus, Mairi would have had a few more hours to deal with her monumentally stupid decision to sleep with Keir. Now she had to deal with Aggie on top of everything else. As she berated herself, her girl parts protested that the decision hadn't been stupid. Her girl parts thought it was the best decision she'd ever made.

Sometimes Mairi hated her girl parts.

Music started outside, and someone began singing another love song.

Mairi groaned and closed her eyes. For a minute there, she'd actually forgotten about the men camped outside her home. Life was closing in on her. Between dealing with losing her sister Isobel to London, having someone hack her life and set her boys on her, and sleeping with Keir—it was all getting a bit too much. It was time to plot an escape. If she climbed out the window and ran, she'd make the ten o'clock bus to Glasgow.

The bedroom door opened, and Agnes stalked in. "Don't even think about it. I know you're in here plotting to run. Just get dressed and get your backside into the living room. This is your mess, but I'm going to help you clean it up." Agnes took the mug from Mairi's hands.

"How do you always know what I'm thinking?" And didn't that just irritate the hell out of her.

"You're painfully transparent," Agnes called as the door slammed behind her.

"Yay for me," Mairi said as she reached for her underwear.

"I hope you know what you're doing," Agnes said to Keir as she came out of the bedroom.

Keir sat at their dining table, drinking coffee and eating the pastries Agnes had brought back from Glasgow. He really needed to get some decent food sometime soon. Something with a vitamin in it would be good. Since moving into Mairi's flat, he'd only eaten junk.

"You back Mairi into a corner and she's liable to make a really stupid decision," Agnes said as she leaned against the kitchen counter. "That's her MO. Dumb decisions made on the spur of the moment under duress."

And didn't he know it. He was hoping that one of those dumb decisions would be to give him a second chance.

"Need more coffee," Mairi announced as she stomped into the room.

Agnes poured a mug and put it on the table beside Keir, while Mairi slumped into a chair. Her hair wasn't so much tied up at the back of her head as it was captured there. It looked like it was working hard to break free and would take over the planet when it did. Mairi, meanwhile, was her usual morning ray of sunshine. She scowled at Keir while she reached for the pastries. She was wearing a pair of faded jeans and a pink t-shirt with the words *You Speak, You Die— You Have Been Warned* on it. Cheery. Keir hid his grin behind his coffee mug.

"What's the big problem?" Mairi said around a mouthful of food.

Agnes stood beside the table, staring down at the two of them, and Keir felt like he was about to be given after-school detention. She folded her arms and tapped her toe while she frowned at them.

"The problem is," she said, "that there are two TV crews set up in the street."

"What?" Keir put down his mug, strode to the window, and pulled back the curtain.

Sure enough, there was a van emblazoned with the Scottish Television logo right in front of his garage, and another one with *BBC Scotland* written on it parked beside the local shop. There were folk with cameras and interviewers with mics talking to Mairi's men, who appeared more than happy to tell them everything they knew. As Keir watched, the woman with Scottish Television tried to interview the Wookiee. It didn't go well.

"What the hell are the TV people doing here?" Keir let the curtain drop and headed back to the table.

"They're saying this is a real-life version of *The Bachelorette*," Agnes said. "They want to cover the process of Mairi choosing a husband and film her announcement of the winner when she reaches a decision. In other words, they want to turn this fiasco into cheap reality TV."

"I need a rope ladder," Mairi said. "Keir, you must have a rope ladder in the garage."

Keir and Agnes stared at her for a moment.

"Aye," Keir said. "Because rope ladders are considered essential equipment for a mechanic."

"You can't run away," Agnes said. "It won't solve anything."

"Are you kidding me?" Mairi said. "It will solve everything. Without me here, there will be no woman to fight over. That means the guys, and the TV crews, will go away. Then, once they're gone, I'll come home and start again."

"Being an online girlfriend?" Keir asked, because he didn't see that happening, now that her reputation had been shot to hell by the hacker.

"There's nothing wrong with being an online girlfriend. It's honest work." She stuck her nose in the air.

"I wasn't saying that. I was wondering how you're going work like usual business when your website is stalled, and you have thirty clients who'll either sign up again with you immediately or drive away your business because you broke their hearts. I'm no judge of good customer service, but running away from the guys who pay you, seems to be on the ill-advised end of the scale."

Mairi blinked at him, then narrowed her eyes. "Why are you still here? Agnes is back. I don't need a bodyguard anymore."

Keir ignored that and took a sip of his coffee. If she thought he was leaving now, she was crazier than he'd ever imagined.

"He's right," Agnes said. "You can't run away. For a start, you don't have the money to live somewhere else for a long period of time, and we have no idea how long these guys will camp out here waiting for you to get back. Secondly, there are TV crews out there. Even if you run, your picture will be plastered all over Scotland, and with that hair, you don't exactly blend with the crowd. As soon as somebody spots you, it will be all over social media that they've found the runaway bachelorette. And then these guys will pack up their caravans and come after you."

"They have to give up at some point," Mairi said, sounding painfully hopeful.

"You said yourself it could take months," Agnes pointed out.

"Yes, but now I'm choosing denial." Mairi reached for another pastry.

"Talk some sense into her," Agnes told Keir.

Keir wasn't sure he was the right man for the job. Sense would mean Mairi never giving him a second chance, because which sensible woman would do that after a guy took her virginity, then walked out on her and straight into prison?

"Rusty, this can be over in ten minutes. All you need to do is marry me."

"I'd rather spend my life as Donald Trump's hairdresser." She glared at him.

"You are deeply disturbed," Keir said.

"That doesn't help!" Agnes threw up her hands in disgust as the front door opened and Donna rushed in.

"I'm going to be on TV." She seemed shocked at the prospect.

Both sisters groaned.

"What did you do?" Agnes demanded as Donna fell onto the couch.

"Nothing." Donna brushed her strawberry blonde hair out of her face. Unlike her sisters, she was dressed in work clothes—gray trousers, black shirt, black shoes. "I just answered the questions they asked me."

"You gave them an interview?" Agnes strode to the sofa to loom over Donna.

Donna's cheeks went red. "They asked me, and I couldn't say no. Honestly, I tried, but the word wouldn't come out of my mouth."

Seeing as Donna was famous for her inability to say no, this was not a surprise to anyone in the room.

"What did they ask you?" Agnes said through clenched teeth.

Donna wet her lips and gave Mairi a nervous glance. "They asked me what Mairi was looking for in a husband."

"And you told them?" Mairi was on her feet. "Couldn't you have said I wasn't looking for one at all and this was one huge, chaotic misunderstanding?"

"Well, yeah." Donna bit her bottom lip. "I suppose I could have."

Keir held up a hand. "Wait. I want to know what you think Mairi is looking for in a husband."

"I, um, was nervous," Donna said, her cheeks even redder now. "I don't know what you want in a husband now. All I could do was tell them what I did know."

Mairi paled and sat back down with a thump. "You didn't."

"What?" Keir and Agnes said in unison.

"I'm sorry, Mairi, I don't deal well with pressure, and there was a camera pointed at me. That made it worse," Donna said.

"What?" Keir and Agnes said, again at the same time, only louder.

Mairi groaned and put her head in her hands. "When we were kids, we wrote lists of all the attributes our perfect husbands would have, and this freak with the perfect memory never bloody forgets these things."

"I am so sorry," Donna said again. "It was the first thing that came to mind."

"I wrote that list when I was thirteen," Mairi wailed.

"Oh, this I've got to hear," Keir said as he folded his arms. He'd given up trying not to grin. This was just too funny.

"Okay," Agnes said. "Everybody get a grip. This can't be too bad. Other than making Mairi look stupid on national TV, there can't be anything on a list written by a thirteen-year-old that will make this situation worse. Right?"

Mairi groaned and rested her forehead on the table.

"What's on the list, Donna?" Keir said through a wide grin.

Donna looked a bit worried about answering, but when Agnes started to tap her toe, she got right to it.

"Good hair, great taste in t-shirts, likes listening to McFly, can sing like Danny Jones, has a dog, plays in a band, buys her chocolate, smart but not a show-off, wants to see the world, is kind and funny and…" She gave Mairi a panicked look.

"Spit it out," Agnes snapped.

"And doesn't pick his nose in public," Donna said in a rush.

"I was thirteen," Mairi said. "There was a boy in my art class who was always picking his nose. It was gross."

Keir grinned at her. "I don't sing like Danny, but I can get a dog, and I never, ever pick my nose in public."

Mairi narrowed her eyes at him, her head still rested on the table. "Why are you still here? Really. I want to know."

"I'm here to protect you from the hordes of McFly fans who're going to rush the building in the hope of convincing you that they'll never pick their noses in public."

"I hate you."

"You'll get over it."

"Okay," Agnes said loudly. "Did you tell the reporter that Mairi wrote the list when she was thirteen?"

"No." Donna's shoulders slumped.

"Did you tell them anything else?" Agnes said.

"No. That was all they asked me." Donna looked up at her sisters. "Should I go downstairs and tell them that was when she was thirteen?"

"No!" three people shouted at once.

The karaoke speaker hissed outside in the street, then squealed loudly, making everyone wince. "Mairi, I want you to know that I never pick my nose. It's unhygienic. You never have to worry about this with me. In the meantime, this one is for you." Then the speaker burst into a bad rendition of McFly's "5 Colours in Her Hair."

"Bet I'm looking pretty damn good round about now," Keir said to Mairi, who closed her eyes and put her arms over her head.

"Make it stop," Mairi shouted.

Agnes stormed to the window, threw it wide and shouted, "Enough!"

There was instant silence. Agnes was about to close the window when a small drone flew through it and headed straight for Mairi. There was a red ribbon attached to the drone, and a small box hung from the ribbon. It floated across the room and hovered over the table where Mairi was still lying with her head under her arms.

"Uh, Rusty, you need to deal with that," Keir said.

She looked up, saw the drone and, with a groan, reached for the box. To no one's surprise, it contained an engagement ring.

"Is that a real diamond?" Agnes said in awe.

"I think so." Mairi looked at her sister. "I get to keep it, right? I mean, even if I say no, I still get to keep it. That's the rule for this proposal thing, isn't it?"

"No." Agnes glared at her. "You don't get to keep it."

Mairi pouted and pulled a note from the box. Keir leaned over to read it.

Marry me. I won't annoy you. John.

"Straight to the point," Keir said. "I like it. He's a keeper."

CHAPTER 17

Of course, being the twenty-first century, the story of Arness' very own bachelorette broke on the internet long before the evening news. Which meant the spectators started to arrive. Mairi looked out of her living room window to find the street in front of the building filled with people—and TV vans. Now there weren't just representatives from Scotland's news, but the breakfast shows had sent staff up from England as well. Edna's shop was doing a roaring trade, and Mairi bet the evil old dragon would try to prolong the siege just to make more cash.

"There are new posts on your Facebook page," Sean said from the dining table behind her.

Seeing as he was the only person she knew locally who had decent computer skills, she'd roped him in to trying to fix the Girlfriend site. So far, he hadn't had any luck either.

"I don't care about the Facebook page," Mairi snapped, her eyes still on her fake boyfriends.

They were up to something. There was a group of them, over at the camping site, with their heads together in a way that made the back of Mairi's neck itch. Definitely plotting, and she'd place a bet on it being something she wasn't going to like.

"You might want to look at this post," Sean said.

Mairi glanced over her shoulder to find him grinning. "What is it?"

"One of the guys made you a website. It's called—wait for it—Marry Me, Mairi."

Mairi hung her head for a minute, while she focused on breathing deeply instead of killing someone, then she stomped over to have a look. Sure enough, there was a whole site dedicated to Sebastian's love for her, including every photo they'd shared since they'd been fake-dating, a page detailing all the things they had in common—*in his head*—a video of him putting on a shadow puppet show about their relationship and a page with an interactive proposal. There were hearts and flowers, but the best touch was the dancing Jedi who wrote the words *Marry Me* with their lightsabers.

"Doesn't anybody ask anymore?" Mairi grumbled. "Marry me isn't even a question. It's an order."

"There's a space for you to type in your answer." Sean pointed at the screen. "What do you want to write?"

She smacked him on the back of the head.

"I'll take that as a no." He typed the word into the heart-shaped box.

As soon as the return key was pressed, the screen went black, then a gif of a young Drew Barrymore crying when she had to say goodbye to ET filled the screen. It kept repeating as the sobbing grew louder.

"I think he's taking it well," Sean said.

"Switch it off." Mairi watched as Sean shut down the website. "Any luck with breaking the hack on the Girlfriend site?"

"Not yet. I'll keep trying. But whoever locked you out knows what they're doing."

"Great." She stalked over to the pile of chocolate boxes, picked one up, ripped into it and started munching.

Agnes, Donna and Keir had all gone to work, leaving Sean to watch over Mairi. Although Keir had reminded her he was downstairs if she needed him.

Which.

She.

Did.

Not.

She plopped back into her old, ratty sofa, clutching the chocolates tightly against her. They were good chocolates, top of the line, straight from Belgium, and she didn't taste a thing as she chomped her way through them. Her brain was too preoccupied with Keir, and nothing else registered, not even the chocolates.

Mairi took a deep breath and admitted the truth to herself—she'd slept with him and it had been her choice. No, that was too tame. She'd had wild, glorious, mind-blowing sex with him—again. And miracles did happen, because he'd still been there the next morning. Only that was a problem now, because she didn't know what to do with him, other than pretend that the night before hadn't happened—which would have been a lot easier if her girl parts didn't start singing the Hallelujah Chorus every time he was within touching distance.

Memories of the days after the last time she'd slept with Keir flashed through her mind, like a movie montage—waking up to find Keir hadn't returned, being unable to contact him, calling his friends and the hospital to make sure he wasn't with either, waiting by the phone to hear from him, and the awful moment when she eventually got a call and her world had collapsed.

She'd walked around in a fog of confusion and disbelief for days, as she tried to get her head around the fact he was awaiting trial. It didn't even make sense. Keir was the best driver she knew. He'd raced cars for years and never had an accident, yet she'd been told that he'd lost control and ended up going through the shop's front window.

She frowned at the memory. "Sean?"

"Aye." He was focused on his laptop.

"The night Keir was arrested, had he been drinking?"

Somehow, it would be even worse if he had. The thought that he'd gone out drinking with his friends after making love to her was just too hurtful to contemplate. She remembered the call he'd gotten, the one that had taken him away from her. It hadn't sounded like a conversation where someone was inviting him out for a night on the town. It had sounded like there was a problem and he'd been called to fix it.

Sean's fingers stopped over the keyboard and his shoulders became rigid. "No. He didn't drink that night."

Exactly what she'd thought. Mairi bit into another chocolate. She hadn't gone to see him when he'd been arrested; she'd been too hurt and angry to face him. Plus, she'd genuinely believed the whole thing would blow over and he'd turn up at her door with a smile and an apology. Whether she would have let him in was another matter, but he'd never turned up for her to find out what she would have done. Instead, she'd read in the local paper that he'd been sent to prison for refusing to tell the police who'd been with him that night. They'd made an example out of him, even though he hadn't committed any crimes as an adult. In effect, he'd chosen his loyalty to his friends over his loyalty to her.

She'd been angry, hurt and confused. She'd also been young and selfish. Now, looking at the events of that night from a distance, and being *slightly* more mature, she might have done things differently. If it happened now, she wouldn't stay home licking her wounds; she would go straight to the police, demand to see him and not leave until Keir gave her an explanation that made sense. Because now that she was looking at things without feeling hurt and furious, she could see that something didn't add up.

"Keir hasn't been in any trouble since that night, has he?" she asked his brother.

"No." Sean seemed frozen in place, as though terrified of what she might ask him next.

That was one thing she could understand. The McKenzie brothers shared the same deep loyalty to each other that she and her sisters shared. Sean probably felt he was betraying his brother by answering Mairi's questions.

"You should ask Keir these questions, not me," he said, confirming her theory.

"Don't worry, I will." Because suddenly she had a whole lot of questions about that night. "But answer this—he'd never been in trouble as an adult, until that night, right?"

"No." Sean was clearly uncomfortable.

Huh. Mairi ate another chocolate. This one was a praline and tasted of nothing, the same as the rest. Apparently Mairi's taste buds and brain couldn't work in tandem, and her brain was definitely working hard—probably for the first time in years—as she puzzled over that night with Keir.

He'd been so careful with her; it had been months before they'd finally slept together. She'd been up-front with him early in their relationship, telling him she'd never had sex but very much wanted to jump his bones. He'd laughed, before his eyes turned dark. "We'll get there, Rusty. Don't you worry."

Mairi's throat tightened, making swallowing the chocolate difficult. For years, she'd thought he hadn't loved her. That he couldn't have loved her if he'd slept with her then fled. But what if there had been more to it? What if he hadn't had a choice?

Instead of working on the jobs that were stacking up, Keir had spent most of his day threatening the people outside his garage to keep them from coming inside. It had turned into a street party. Folk turned up with picnics, there was music playing over at the geek campsite, and the reporters interviewed anyone who stood still long enough. The quiet village of Arness had become a mecca for geeks and gawkers. On top of that, the deliveries for Mairi just kept on coming. The latest one was the most worrying of all.

"Is that what I think it is?" Hamish said as he wiped his already clean hands on a rag and stared at the large box addressed to Mairi.

Keir could never figure out how the man managed to do a full day's work in the garage and not get even a drop of oil on him.

"I really hope not," Keir said.

The box was big, as in refrigerator-sized big, and printed on the front was the name of a well-known adult toy store.

"Looks to me like someone sent her one of those life-sized sex dolls," Hamish said.

And damned if it didn't look exactly the same way to Keir, which made his skin feel like beetles were crawling all over it. There were good gifts and then there were funny gifts—this was neither. This was just disturbing.

"In my day," Hamish said, "we sent flowers. If we were serious, jewelry. I once sent a woman a really nice handbag. She hit me with it when she dumped me."

There was really nothing to say to that. "I'm not carrying this upstairs. I feel like I need a bath just looking at it."

"I've got a car to fix," Hamish said as he headed for the Mini Cooper that was blocking the entrance to the garage.

"Coward," Keir called after him as he pulled his phone from his back pocket and called Mairi.

"That isn't funny," she said as soon as she answered.

"What isn't?" Keir grinned. He knew exactly what she was talking about.

"Setting your ringtone to the 'Wedding March.'"

"It's only a matter of time, Rusty. I'm irresistible and you're backed against the wall."

"Never give up, never surrender."

She was even beginning to sound like her fan club. "That's a sci-fi quote, right? Never mind. I called for a reason. There's another delivery down here for you." He eyed the box with disgust.

"Can't you just bring it up?" she whined. "I'm busy."

"Doing what? Hiding?"

"And eating chocolate. Come on, Keir, bring the box up for me."

"Nope. There's no way I'm touching this."

There was a pause as her tiny brain worked things out. "Sounds good. I'll be right down."

"You might want to take a minute to clean up. Your camera crew is hovering."

"They aren't my camera crew, Keir."

He snorted a laugh and hung up. Mairi would do what she wanted to do—as usual.

When the door to the stairs to Mairi's apartment opened a minute later, Keir knew she hadn't bothered to take his advice. She bounced toward him, with her hair corralled in a massive scrunchie, wearing her old jeans, her *Don't Talk* t-shirt and a pair of old, fluffy bunny slippers. She definitely hadn't dressed for the cameras, and all Keir could think was that he wished they were still together in bed.

"What is it?" Mairi rounded a car, tripped over his toolbox and fell into him.

Keir put his arms around her to hold her upright, and just like that, the chemistry between them ignited. Her fingers flexed on his biceps and big eyes looked up at him with heated speculation.

"You keep looking at me like that, Rusty, and we're going to put on a different kind of show for the cameras."

Her eyes darkened, and she looked like she was actually considering it. Ah, hell. He backed her into the tiny corridor leading to the bathroom and pressed her against the wall. He didn't give her time to think; he just cupped her face and indulged them both in a slow, lazy kiss. She melted in his arms, and Keir wished he was alone with her, instead of skulking in his garage with the world outside his door. Alone, he could push his luck with her, but here, he had to hold back and exercise patience.

Patience sucked.

He stepped away from Mairi, instantly feeling the loss, and watched as her cheeks turned his favorite shade of pink.

There was a strange vulnerability in her eyes. One he'd never seen before. It made him want to stand between her and the world, vowing to keep her safe. There was only problem with that: who would keep her safe from him?

"I thought one night would get it out of my system," she said softly, oblivious to the ammunition she'd just handed him.

Ammunition he would never use against her. Instead, he reached out and ran his fingertips down her cheek. "Even if we'd had a million nights, it still wouldn't be out of our systems."

Mairi swallowed hard and tore her eyes from him. "Where's this delivery you don't want to touch?"

"Over there." Reluctantly, he stepped out of the corridor and pointed to the corner beside the open garage doors.

When Mairi appeared beside him, the vultures scented blood and started to circle.

"Mairi Sinclair," a reporter shouted, "can you tell us a little about your motivation in setting up a boyfriend competition?"

"There was no motivation," Mairi shouted back. "I was hacked. This is someone's idea of a joke."

The crowd laughed, clearly thinking she was playing with them.

"Why won't they believe me?" Mairi said to Keir.

He shrugged. "People are nuts."

"There is that." She strode over to the box and stood in front of it.

Keir followed, shouting out a reminder to the crowd that if they stepped through his doorway, he was calling the cops. They backed off.

"Please tell me one of those lunatics didn't buy me a sex doll," Mairi said as he came to a stop beside her. Close beside her, with their sides touching, because he couldn't stand next to Mairi and not touch her.

He cocked an eyebrow at her in reply. There was no telling what a desperate geek would do.

"They wouldn't, right?" Mairi said. "I mean, logic would say that if you planned to marry someone, there would be no need for them to have a sex doll."

"Logic would, aye, but I'm not sure your guys are capable of normal logic."

Mairi studied the box for a minute, as though she'd develop x-ray vision if she stared at it long enough.

"I can't open it down here, not with the cameras. Help me get it upstairs." She did that innocent eyelash-flapping thing she did when she wanted to get her own way.

It didn't work. "I don't want to touch it." He took a step back.

"Stop being a wuss and give me a hand."

"Nope."

"Come on, Keir, this isn't funny. Help me get this out of here. They're getting closer."

He looked behind them, and sure enough, the crowd was inching as close as they could without Keir calling the cops. There were even one or two people holding up phones to film their exchange.

"Keir," she said out of the corner of her mouth. "Help me. Now."

And that was when it came to him. "I'll do it for a price."

She narrowed her eyes. "What do you want?"

He took a step closer to her and lowered his head to hers. She smelled like she'd rolled around in a strawberry patch. It made him want to cover her in cream and lick it all off. "I want you to ride with me."

She sucked in a breath and her cheeks turned pink again, making him think he wasn't the only one who wanted to experiment with cream.

"Not that kind of ride." Keir stroked his hand down her arm and watched her shiver. "The kind that takes place on the back of my bike." He stepped even closer until they were touching again. "Although I certainly wouldn't say no to the other kind."

Keir missed their bike rides, and he was betting Mairi did too. After an hour wrapped around him, with the machine throbbing between her thighs, she'd been all over him like chocolate sauce on ice cream, and it had taken all of Keir's self-control to keep things slow between them. Back then, the last thing he'd wanted was to take Mairi, for their first time, on the dirt beside his bike. Now, that sounded like a great idea.

From the way her breath sped up and she bit her lip, she knew her memories had gone exactly where he wanted them to. "Fine, I'll go for a bike ride with you. Now help me lift this."

It was hard not to kiss her again, in full view of everyone. "Your wish is my command." He tipped the box toward her and bent down to lift the bottom.

Mairi grabbed the top. "This is lighter than I thought it would be. It can't be a doll."

"Could be a blow-up," Keir said.

They slowly hefted the box through the garage, stepping over car parts and around waiting vehicles. They were almost at the stairs when Mairi tripped. She let go of the box, grabbing a nearby shelf to steady herself—and the box hit the floor and split.

Flashes went off, and the blinding light from the TV set-up filled the garage. Gasps and giggles were all they could hear while their eyesight adjusted, and then Keir looked down to find the floor strewn with clothes. Kinky clothes. Someone had bought every sexy dress-up outfit they could get their hands on. There was an itty-bity nurse costume, a slinky black leather cat suit, a maid's uniform, a pirate costume, a harem outfit, a policewoman costume and some other outfits he didn't recognize. There was also a selection of headbands with ears, fluffy handcuffs and what looked like a rider's crop.

Keir vowed there and then to track down the guy who'd sent her this present and beat him into next week. "This isn't romantic. This is just wrong."

Mairi picked up the black cat suit and held it at arm's length, to get a good look at it. A beaming smile lit up her face. "This. Is. Awesome!" she said.

Keir rubbed a hand over his face. Of course, she liked the kinky gift.

"Do you think I could wear this out, like, normally?" she asked. "I would totally rock it."

Keir was saved from answering, as Hamish came around the car to see what was happening.

"You might want to check out the rear view before you get too excited," Hamish said.

Mairi turned the cat suit. There was a hole where the backside should be.

She blinked at it. "That looks cold," she said.

Keir let out another groan.

CHAPTER 18

Mairi ordered delivery pizzas for dinner, and when they arrived, the teenage boy opened a box lid and grinned at her. He'd scrawled the words *Marry me instead of them* on the card.

"Very funny." She took the pizzas from him and slammed the door in his face.

"Another admirer?" Keir said from where he was lounging on the couch.

He hadn't bothered to ask anyone if he was invited to dinner. He'd just walked up the stairs at the end of his workday and made himself comfortable on the couch. Strangely, it seemed perfectly normal to have him there.

"A joker." Mairi handed the pizzas to Agnes, who put them on their coffee table.

They were gathered around the TV, waiting for the evening news. To irritate Keir, because she'd known there was no stopping him from coming upstairs after work, Mairi had changed into the cat suit. The hole was covered by a pair of cut-off jeans she'd pulled on over the suit, and on her head she wore a black headband, complete with cat ears. From the looks she was getting, Keir didn't know if he was turned on at the sight, or deeply repelled by the fact she was wearing a costume another man had sent her. Mairi swung her hips and grinned. Driving Keir mad was a whole lot of fun.

"So, who gave you the costumes?" Keir said at last, and Mairi wondered if his tiny brain hurt from keeping the question trapped inside for so long.

She beamed at him from where she was grabbing napkins and plates from the kitchen. "The twins. I think it was Darius' idea, because Damien would never have thought of it. Damien would probably have sent me a state-of-the-art pocket calculator. Although, I could be wrong. He does do all that sport stuff and has the abs of a god." She gave Keir a wistful look, as though she deeply regretted not getting her hands on those abs. Which, to be honest, she kind of did.

Keir made a little growling sound and ripped his shirt off over his head. "You call those abs? *These* are abs." He pointed at his flat, ripped stomach, just in case there was any confusion.

"Put your shirt back on," Agnes snapped from her seat at the dining table. "The news is starting."

Agnes turned up the volume as the evening news anchor started her intro, and a scowling Keir pulled his shirt back on. Mairi ambled over to stand beside the sofa, and Keir reached up, grabbed her wrist and pulled her down beside him. She frowned at him, but didn't move away, which seemed to calm his jealous beast some.

"You might think that the *Bachelor* and *Bachelorette* series only happen on TV," the news anchor said, "but in the small town of Arness, one local woman is living the premise *without* the cameras. Here's our reporter with more."

The female reporter Keir had barked at repeatedly, filled the screen. "I'm in Arness, in the Kintyre peninsula. Where twenty-three men have turned up from all over the world to try to win the hand of Mairi Sinclair, after she posted online that she was looking for a husband.

"The men are already known to Mairi, as they form part of the client list she has as an online girlfriend. Here to explain is one of Mairi's boyfriends, Sebastian Mark." She turned to a smiling Sebastian. "Tell us more about this online girlfriend arrangement you have with Mairi."

While Sebastian explained, Mairi looked up at Keir. "I think this was taped before I said no to his website marriage proposal. Although, I don't think he was heartbroken when he was rejected, either. I don't think any of these guys really want to marry me, and I'm totally okay with that."

"So am I," he said darkly, proving the jealous beast was still lurking.

"As you can see," the reporter said as the TV switched to a live shot of her outside the local shop, "the men are gearing up for another evening of stunts, in an attempt to attract the attention of Mairi Sinclair. In fact, one of the men has a special display for Mairi, which is starting as we speak. Mairi, if you're watching, this is from Jonas."

The camera swung to show the Wookiee on the grass verge at the edge of the cliff. He was lighting a huge fireworks display he'd set up, part of which was a massive wooden stand with fireworks strapped to it in the shape of letters. It was too dark to see what the letters spelled out, but it didn't take a genius to work out it was another marriage proposal.

As the screen cut away from Arness, and the anchor continued with the rest of the news, Mairi rushed to the window. Fireworks filled the sky and dazzled everyone who watched them. But Mairi wasn't watching the sky; she was watching the idiot Wookiee, who was standing far too close to the firework message he was about to light. With a squeal, she turned and ran for the door.

"What is it?" Keir called as he jumped up to follow.

"The Wookiee's flammable," Mairi shouted over her shoulder.

She flew down the stairs at the back of their building and ran through the crowd to get to Jonas. Keir sped up and ran in front of her, elbowing folk out of the way to clear a path for her. For once, Mairi wished she didn't have such short legs and could run faster. Short but perfect legs, she mentally amended.

"He's lighting the words," Mairi shouted at Keir. "You have to stop him. He's too close."

Keir put on a burst of speed, but it was too late. The fireworks that made up the words sparked to life. The sparks caught the acrylic hair of the Wookiee costume. And Jonas went up in flames.

Mairi screamed. Keir didn't hesitate. He tackled Jonas, taking him to the grass and rolling the big guy around like he was a toddler. The crowd went eerily silent as Mairi fell to her knees beside Jonas and Keir.

"Jonas?" She wasn't sure where to touch him, but she wanted to pat him and let him know it would be okay. "Jonas, speak to me. How bad is it?"

"You," Keir snapped at a guy beside him. "Call an ambulance."

The guy hurried to do as he was told. Around them, people were too busy using their phones to video the disaster, to call for help. Mairi wanted to slap each and every one of them.

"Jonas, please talk to me." She wiped a tear from her cheek.

Huge chunks of the costume were black and melted, but

his hands were still okay. So Mairi wrapped the nearest one tight in hers.

The Wookiee stirred. "Don't cry," came a very human voice from his hairy mouth.

"Once we get you checked out, I am going to shout at you for a week. What were you thinking?"

"Wasn't," he said.

"Leave the telling off for later," Keir said softly as a siren was heard in the distance.

Behind him, the words Jonas had written blazed to life: *Will You Marry Me?*

"At last," Mairi said as she wiped away the tears. "Someone who understands it's a question."

Around them, Mairi's fake boyfriends gathered. They kept the crowd back, and they closed in around Jonas, offering support with their presence. When the ambulance arrived, Keir explained the situation to the accompanying police officer as Mairi stood silently weeping. This whole situation had gotten completely out of hand, and now someone was hurt.

"He'll be okay," Sebastian said, putting a hesitant hand on her shoulder.

Mairi turned to him and hugged him tight. Behind her, Amir rubbed her back and the twins came up beside them. Although she felt nothing romantic for her men, and she was equally sure they didn't feel that way about her, it didn't mean she didn't care for them. They were like her pets. A whole heap of clueless puppies who needed her to survive the world.

"This has to stop," Mairi said against Sebastian's chest. "People are getting hurt."

"Does she need chocolate?" Amir asked someone. "I can get her some."

"I think she needs to cry," Damien said. "I read about this

—women like to get their emotions out. It's good for them. If they don't, they get blocked, or something."

Mairi looked up in time to see Darius smack his brother across the back of his head. "Idiot," he said.

It made Mairi smile through her tears. As she listened to the ambulance drive off, the group around her parted and Keir appeared. She didn't know why she did it, but she turned from Sebastian's arms and straight into his. He held her tight, as she'd known he would.

"He's going to be fine." Keir kissed the top of her head. "You want to go to the hospital?"

Mairi nodded against his chest.

"You guys coming?" Keir said to the other men.

"We'll clean up here," Darius said, "then we'll come on over. Somebody needs to get rid of this crowd."

"Haul in the cop," Keir said. "He's my cousin. He'll help you clear the place out."

"Your cousin?" Mairi looked up at him. How had she missed that news?

"Not one you know, big ears. I'll introduce you later. Come on, let's go see the Wookiee."

"Wait," Sebastian said. "Jonas won't be comfortable without a costume to wear once he's released from hospital. I don't have anything that will fit him." He looked at the other guys.

"I've got a Batman costume with me," Damien said, making his brother groan. "He can have that."

Sebastian let out a relieved sigh. "We'll bring it with us when we come."

As they walked away, with Mairi tucked under Keir's arm, she looked at the sign that had almost killed Jonas.

"This has to end," she told Keir.

"You know what to do," he said. "One little announcement and this all goes away."

For the first time since he'd offered to marry her, it didn't seem like such a terrible idea. Not for her sake, she quickly told herself, but to end the hysteria. As she mulled it over, she let Keir fit a motorcycle helmet on her head, and then she climbed onto his bike behind him.

It was like coming home.

CHAPTER 19

Keir sat in the waiting room of Campbeltown's small hospital, beside an unusually subdued Mairi, and worried over her silence. She was obviously thinking, which boded ill for everyone around her—especially him.

Throughout the waiting room, the rest of the fake boyfriends sat wherever they could find space. With the exception of Darius, every single one of the guys had a phone, iPad or laptop in their hands. For some reason, Keir wanted to take away their toys and make them do something more productive with their time. It was almost as though they'd activated his dormant parental gene, and he had to wonder when he'd stopped looking at them as rivals and started looking at them as clueless kids. Hell, these *men* were nobody's kids; half of them were older than Keir. Still, he couldn't quite shake the feeling that he had to sort them out.

A smiling, middle-aged nurse came out of the emergency room, scanned the waiting crowd and made a beeline for Mairi. "So you're the famous bachelorette."

"Not because I want to be," Mairi grumbled. "What's happening with Jonas?"

The woman's face softened, making her seem years younger. "He's fine. The damage was minimal." She looked at Keir. "Mainly because you got to him quickly, but also because he was fully dressed under his Care Bear suit."

"Wookiee," Sebastian said. "He was a Wookiee."

The nurse shook her head in bewilderment. "Anyway, he was wearing jeans and a long-sleeved cotton shirt. That's what saved him from getting badly burned. Although the costume was made of plastic fibers, he had a layer of natural material underneath, which protected him."

"So, he doesn't have any burns?" Mairi asked.

But Keir knew better. He'd seen burns victims before. He put his arm around her shoulders and pulled her tight against him. For some strange reason, the fake boyfriends smiled at him, instead of looking daggers at him for touching their woman. If he lived to be a hundred, he would never figure those guys out.

"No," the nurse said. "He has burns. They just aren't as bad as they could have been. He'll be in pain, and we need to keep him cool and hydrated while he heals, so we're moving him to the burns unit in Glasgow."

"Oh." Another tear ran down Mairi's cheek. "Can we see him?"

"Sure." The nurse looked around the room. "Let's keep it to a couple of people at a time, though."

Mairi and Keir stood, and so did Sebastian. His face fell when he saw Keir was going in with Mairi.

"Three's okay, right?" Keir asked the nurse.

She smiled. "Three is fine."

"Come on," Keir said to Sebastian. "Let's go see how the idiot is doing."

"The *idiot* has two PhDs and made several million dollars last year from a piece of software he designed," Sebastian said.

"Seriously?" Keir said. "And he wants to marry Mairi?"

She smacked him in the stomach, but stayed under his arm, as they went through the door to visit Jonas. When Keir saw him, he almost took a step back. His face hadn't suffered any burns, unlike his body. But that wasn't what made Keir do a double take. Jonas the Wookiee looked like he'd fallen out of a *GQ* photo spread and straight into Campbeltown hospital. The guy would have given Brad Pitt a run for his money any day of the week. And this was hidden under a Wookiee suit? Keir *really* didn't understand these guys.

"Jonas," Mairi said as she rushed to his side.

For the first time since this boyfriend situation started, Keir felt a genuine pang of worry. Jonas had everything— looks, intellect, money. How was a guy supposed to compete with that?

"He's really shy," Sebastian said softly from Keir's side. "Don't growl at him. He doesn't need the extra stress, and he hasn't got his Wookiee head to hide under."

That was when Keir's shoulders relaxed, because even with everything Jonas had, he was still a guy with problems —just like the rest of them.

Keir watched as Mairi brushed Jonas' blond hair from his forehead with one hand and clung to his hand with the other.

"Are you in a lot of pain?" she said.

The guy flushed a deep red when he glanced at her, then answered the bedding instead of Mairi. "They've given me drugs. I feel okay. Maybe a little dumb."

"They're moving you to Glasgow," Mairi said as Keir came to stand beside her. "I don't know how long you'll be in hospital, but we'll visit you there. Should we contact your family?"

"I already did," Sebastian said from the other side of the bed. "They're waiting for word on whether they should come over from Canada. They want to know what Jonas wants them to do."

Keir reeled at the thought of being in hospital and his family not rushing to his bedside.

Jonas glanced up at Sebastian. "Can you tell them to wait? And thank them for asking. I know it's hard on Mom."

"Sure thing." Sebastian pulled out his phone and started texting. "Your mom was upset. She said she can be here the minute you say the word."

"I know," Jonas said, but you could tell it would be too much for him. Which made Keir feel bad for the family who obviously wanted to be with their son.

"Jonas," Mairi said, "I can't shout at you right now, because I'm too happy you're going to be okay. But I want you to know, I'm saving it up for when you're better."

Jonas' lips quirked and a small smile broke free as he stared at the bedding. "I didn't get an answer to my question, Mairi."

Mairi stilled, and for the first time since the geeks arrived in town determined to make her marry one of them, Keir realized rejecting the men hurt her. They were her friends, people she'd come to know through years of interacting online and hurting them was making her suffer. He put a hand on her shoulder and gave a gentle squeeze. If he ever got his hands on the hacker who started this, he was going to pummel them into the dirt.

"The answer's no, Jonas," Mairi said softly. "But I promise you this—if it's the last thing I do, I will find you—and Sebastian—lovely women for you to marry."

"You don't need to do that," Jonas mumbled.

Sebastian's head snapped up from his phone. "Yes, she does. She totally does. Can I put in an order? I'd like someone blonde, with blue eyes and freckles. She has to understand *Star Trek* and anime and have a good sense of humor."

"Dude," Jonas said, "you asked a redhead who doesn't like anime to marry you."

"Oh." Sebastian's head went red. "Of course, you will always be the standard by which I measure other women. That's why I want a blonde. No bad memories associated with the hair color."

Mairi threw back her head and laughed. "I'll see what I can do."

The nurse poked her head into the room. "You about done? There's a whole crowd out here itching to get to our boy."

"Yes, we're done for now." Mairi leaned over and placed a gentle kiss on Jonas' cheek, and, for a second, Keir thought the guy was going to pass out.

"You coming?" Keir said to Sebastian.

"No. I'll stay with Jonas and go with him to Glasgow. We're in the middle of a game of Dungeons & Dragons that should keep us busy while he recovers."

Keir just shook his head.

"You get better, okay? You mean a lot to me," Mairi said over her shoulder. "Both of you do."

Keir put his hand on the small of her back, feeling the ridiculous pleather cat suit under his touch and noting that Mairi was still wearing the matching ears. They said good-night to the rest of her men and headed out to the carpark. When Keir lifted the helmet to put it on her head, Mairi stilled him with a touch. Big blue eyes peered up at him, filled to overflowing with weariness.

"I don't want to go back to the flat tonight," she said. "There will still be a crowd, and maybe TV people too. I need space to think."

"Where do you want to go, Rusty?" He'd take her anywhere she wanted to be.

"Can we go to your place?" There was a vulnerability in the question that he never would have expected from his Rusty. The events of the evening had knocked her usual sparkle right out of her.

"Course we can."

When she relaxed, he realized she'd been expecting him to say no, and that made his heart clench tight. He fitted the helmet over her crazy headband, climbed on his bike and waited for Mairi to climb on behind him. She snuggled up close, the way he'd taught her to years earlier, wrapped her arms around his middle and held on tight.

As soon as she'd settled, Keir started the bike and headed for his house on the outskirts of Campbeltown. The house he'd bought two years earlier with the hope that, one day, Mairi would live in it with him.

CHAPTER 20

Mairi was in a strange mood. It wasn't one she often experienced, because she didn't usually spend time plagued by deep thoughts. But as she rode behind Keir, it felt like her thoughts were pressing down on her, with a weight that made her wonder if she would ever stand again.

Keir had been right when he told her she was backed into a corner. With the media interested in her story, and her fake boyfriends pulling increasingly crazy stunts to "win" the game, there were very few options left for her to put a stop to the husband competition. In fact, as time went on, it seemed like she really only had two options to get out of the mess she was in—run away, or marry Keir.

Keir.

She felt like a dam had burst within her when it came to Keir, and she was drowning in the confusing emotions, needs, and fears that swamped her. In only a few days, she'd gone from angrily keeping her distance, to leaning on him for the strength she needed to figure things out. Not only that, but she'd fallen straight into bed with the man she swore she'd never touch again. And she'd loved it.

Everything was mixed up in her head. Now that she'd started touching him, she seemed unable to stop. Every time he was near her, she wanted to pull him to her and do wicked, wicked things that would leave him panting for more. When he entered a room, it was as though he was the only person she could see. The air between them became electric and Mairi's body started screaming for more. Her body desperately wanted Keir, but her mind wasn't so sure. She still had questions about the night he'd walked out on her. Questions she wasn't sure she was ready to have answered.

And then there was trust.

How could she trust the man who'd left her after he'd made her love him? How could she trust him not to do it again? She'd watched her parents repeat the same cycle of abuse and forgiveness for twenty-six years, to the point where the sisters not only didn't respect them, they weren't even sure they loved them anymore. If she let Keir back in, would they turn into her parents? Would he hurt her yet again? Would she make excuses for him, allowing the cycle to repeat continuously?

She didn't know.

But she was beginning to think the point was moot, because she was afraid she was falling in love with the man all over again. It was a terrifying possibility, because love hurt. It broke you and left you bleeding. It could not be trusted.

Even knowing all this, she was fairly certain marrying Keir was her only option if she wanted to get out of the mess she was in. It was either that or walk away, with nothing in her pocket and even less in the bank, to try to build her life anew somewhere else—an impossible feat.

If ever there was a stupid decision waiting to be made, this was it.

When Keir pulled the bike up in front of a small stone house, it took Mairi a few seconds to realize they'd stopped —she was that deep in thought.

He squeezed her hand. "Come on, Rusty. I'll show you around."

Mairi climbed off the bike and let Keir take the helmet from her head. All the while, her eyes were on the house. Somehow she'd pictured him in a flat in the center of town, not in a white cottage on the outskirts. She looked behind her, and sure enough, there was the loch, black in the night, but reflecting the street lights on the opposite side of the water.

Keir tugged her hand, and she followed him up the three steps and through the wide oak door. She ran her fingers over the stained glass panel beside the door.

"You have stained glass," she said inanely.

"Came with the house," he said gruffly. "You must be cold. You weren't wearing a jacket on the bike."

As he said it, Mairi's skin began to chill, and she wrapped her arms around her middle. "I didn't notice."

He opened the door to a closet that was just inside the entrance and brought out a fleece-lined hoodie. "Let's get you into this."

She obediently let him wrap her up in the top, waiting while he zipped it up and rolled up her sleeves. "Thanks."

He cupped the back of her neck. "I don't like it when you're quiet. Usually, I'd worry that you were plotting something I'd regret, but this feels different, and I don't know what to do to make it better."

There was nothing he could do. The decision she had to make was one only she could work out.

"Show me your house," she told him. "Then make me a nice warm cup of tea."

Keir gave her a worried look before he took her hand and

led her along the polished wooden floorboards of his hallway. The wooden floor extended into his living room, which contained a big black leather sofa, a steel and glass coffee table and a giant TV. There were no curtains on the windows, and the view over the loch during the day would be stunning.

"I see you decorated in twentieth-century guy." Mairi pointed at the wall where there was a framed print of a red car she couldn't identify. If it wasn't driven by Doc Brown or Marty McFly, she didn't have a clue what it was. "Even down to the artwork."

"Come on, smart-arse." He tugged her hand, and she trailed after him.

The house was small, but gorgeous. Keir had painted the walls white and left the wood natural and polished. At some point, someone had obviously converted the attic to extra rooms, and there was a narrow staircase leading up to them from the end of the hallway. They skipped the stairs and turned right, into the kitchen.

"The bathroom is on the other side of the stairs," Keir said. "Next to it's a bedroom I use to store my workout equipment."

"That explains the abs."

"The abs are natural, Rusty. I was born with them. Don't you remember?" His eyes sparkled at her, and she felt her cheeks flush.

She did remember seeing them often while they were dating, but she didn't remember them being quite so spectacular. She looked around the kitchen, which sported granite countertops, black breakfast-bar stools and stainless steel appliances.

"What do men have against color?" Mairi asked as she climbed onto a stool.

Keir filled the silver kettle from the tap over the butler's sink. Mairi had always wanted a butler's sink, and a kitchen island—just like the one she was sitting at. Although, if this were her house, there would be a whole lot more color.

"I suppose you'd fill the place with flowers and colored cushions," Keir said with a smile.

"Keir, I've seen three pictures on your walls, and they are all of cars." She pointed at the one above the large wooden dining table. "And that one is gray."

"Point taken," he said. "You hungry?"

"I could eat cake," she said hopefully.

"No cake, but I have ice cream."

Mairi shook her head. She was cold enough without adding to it. "I'll just take tea."

While he made her a cup, she glanced over at his back door and noticed there was a massive pet door cut into it.

"You have a dog door," she said.

"Last owners had a Doberman, which means I'm all set up for that list of yours. All I need to do is get a dog—and take some singing lessons."

He put a mug of nice, strong, milky tea in front of her, before leaning on the island opposite her. "What you going to do about this mess, Rusty?"

She sipped at her tea while she watched him. "I need time to think about it."

"Time is running out. People are getting hurt."

"Just tonight, Keir. Let me have tonight. I'll make a decision tomorrow."

He looked at her for the longest time before his face softened and he pushed away from the counter. "Okay, gorgeous, we won't talk about it tonight." He turned his back to her as he filled another mug with steaming water. "You want to watch a movie before going to bed?"

Mairi watched his shoulders move and his back ripple. Her eyes trailed down to his narrow hips and those thick, solid thighs. Everything about him called to her. As soon as she'd set eyes on him, she'd wanted to touch, to lose herself in him, and now she felt exactly the same. She wanted to spend the night losing herself in Keir and forget about everything else. It was selfish and cruel; she didn't want to lead him on when she wasn't even sure what she was thinking or feeling.

"Rusty?"

Her name snapped her out of her thoughts, and she realized Keir had come around the counter to stand beside her.

"What's going on?" He reached out and ran his hand down her arm to hold her hand.

Her skin burned where he touched her, and every fiber of her being reached for him.

"I'm being selfish and trying not to be. It's hard. I'm not used to thinking about anyone other than me."

"How are you being selfish?" His brow furrowed.

She tore her eyes from his and looked around. "I came here because I'm hiding from my mess. I'm leaning on you when I know it only confuses things between us, and…" She shook her head. "Never mind."

"Tell me," he whispered as he clasped her chin gently and turned her face to his. "It's okay. Just tell me."

She saw that look in his eyes again. The one that thrilled and terrified her in equal measure. The one that said Keir felt a whole lot more for her than he was letting on. The one that promised he could love her, if she would only let him.

It was a reason not to tell him what she wanted. A good reason. And yet, her selfish, longing heart and her needy, lonely body wouldn't let her keep her mouth closed.

"I want to go upstairs," she whispered.

His hand tightened on hers. "Rusty?"

"I want to spend the night forgetting. With you. I want you. Tonight." She looked away. "I don't know about tomorrow, Keir, and I know I'm being selfish asking for this." She gave a dry chuckle. "I've been thinking about myself for so long that it's hard to stop doing it, but I'm trying."

Keir reached out and removed the mug from her hand. "It isn't selfish if I want it too."

Her heart stopped in her chest.

"Come on," he said.

He tugged her hand, and she let him pull her off the stool. Then, in silence, she followed him upstairs to his bedroom.

CHAPTER 21

Keir wasn't sure what was going on. Mairi wasn't herself: she was confused and hurting. Her whole world had turned upside down, and she didn't know how to fix it. He understood what she meant about using him, but he didn't feel the same way about things. If he could give her a few hours of pleasure, of respite from the thoughts driving her nuts, then he was more than happy to do so. Even more than that, he wanted to be with Mairi. He wanted to show her, through every touch, how much she meant to him and how desperately he wanted to be with her.

He wasn't an idiot. Their relationship, if you could even call it that, was balanced on the edge of a knife. One false move and they'd both be bleeding. Even knowing that, he couldn't stop the hope rising inside him, because Mairi was here, in his house, soon to be in his bed. After years of dismissing him, she was touching him, talking to him, leaning on him. It was more than he'd ever hoped to achieve in such a short period, and nothing would stop him from showing her how much he loved her. That he'd never stopped loving her. That he would always love her. He was born to love Mairi, and everything within him ached when she wouldn't let him.

He pushed his bedroom door open, realizing his bed wasn't made and that Mairi wouldn't even notice, which made him smile.

"More gray and black, Keir? Really?"

He smiled at her. "Tell you what. You marry me. and you can flood the house with color."

"Funny," she said, but before she looked away, he saw only pain in her eyes.

"Hey. I was joking."

"I know." Her eyes were shuttered now, and he couldn't read them. "Do you know what's really funny?"

"Tell me," he said, hoping she didn't mean that ironically, because if she told him something sad and burst into tears, he didn't know what he would do.

This time when she looked up at him, her smile was genuine. "I'm wearing this stupid cat suit, and I don't think I can get out of it. I had to use half a bottle of baby oil to get into it."

His heart stuttered, and his cock woke up from its slumber. "Putting aside the thought of you and a bottle of baby oil, why did you put the damn thing on?" It still rankled that she was wearing a sexy outfit some other guy had sent her.

"I put it on to wind you up." Her grin was pure mischief. "It worked."

He narrowed his eyes. "Then you won't care if the suit doesn't survive me taking it off."

"You wouldn't." She took a step back.

"Oh, yes, I definitely would." He lunged for her, but she squealed and ran, scrambling over the bed to the other side.

"Come on," she said, "even the bedding is gray."

He threw himself over the bed at her, but she laughed and ran, letting him land with a thump on the floor. She was heading for the door, but Keir was faster; he snagged her ankle, making her fall in front of him.

"That's cheating," she said.

"I didn't know there were rules." He held her tight as he crawled over her to straddle her hips.

"Now, Keir. This was a gift. You need to be reasonable. It isn't polite to ruin other people's gifts." There was no sadness in her eyes now. They sparkled with mischief. The wild woman he knew and loved was well and truly back, and he was going to make sure she stayed for good.

He grabbed the neckline of the suit and pulled. Nothing happened. He'd expected it to rip, but all it did was stretch.

"What the hell?"

"It's indestructible," Mairi said through laughter. "I'll have to live in it forever, which makes me thankful for the missing bum section." She dissolved into hysterics.

"Stay here." Keir climbed off her. "I'm serious. Don't move. I'll be right back."

She was still laughing when he ran down the stairs to find some scissors. That cat suit was coming off, even if he had to shred it.

When he got back, Mairi had moved. She was in his closet, going through his clothes. She stuck her head out to look at him. "Even ninety percent of your clothing is black or gray. You need counseling." She spotted the scissors in his hand and her eyebrows shot up her forehead. "Oh hell no, you're not getting near me with scissors."

And she ran for it. Again. This time, he was ready for her and faked her out when she scrambled over the bed. Instead of going over it after her, he rounded it and hooked an arm around her waist. With one swift move, he tossed her into the middle of the bed, then tumbled her to her belly.

"Don't move," he said. "I have scissors, and I don't want to cut you."

She froze. "You cut me, you die."

"That's fair." He put the scissors on the bed beside them and yanked her denim shorts over her hips and down her legs.

His heart almost stopped completely at the sight of the creamy, succulent cheeks peeking out of all that black. He ran his hands over her flesh and squeezed, delighting when Mairi let out a little moan.

"I've think I've changed my mind," he said. "Maybe we should keep this outfit."

"I'm glad you've come around to my way of thinking. Every time I look at it, I think of the twins, and I wouldn't want to lose that precious memory."

"This sucker has to die." Keir reached for the scissors and straddled Mairi's thighs, to keep her from moving suddenly and injuring herself.

He gripped the material in the gap at the bottom of her back and cut into it. It took some force, but he managed to cut a line straight up her back to her neck. The material fell apart, and Mairi heaved a sigh of relief.

"That was *not* comfortable," she said.

Keir was too distracted to pay attention to her words. He put the scissors down for a second to run his hands over her beautiful, plump behind and up her smooth back.

"You are so soft."

"That will be the baby oil."

He grinned as he stroked her flesh. "You know, I think I'm kinkier than I realized, because cutting you out of this thing is making me a little desperate."

"Then have at it," she said, her voice husky. "The sleeves pinch."

"Then they have to go." He picked up the scissors and cut a line up each sleeve.

"Better," she said on a sigh.

Keir moved down to her legs and cut the suit away from each one, starting at her hip and working his way down the outside of each thigh. At last, the suit lay in pieces beneath her.

"You aren't wearing any underwear." He sounded guttural as he ran his hands from her ankles, up her legs and over her body.

"You saw the suit. There wasn't room for underwear."

The breathless words made him want to hit every man who'd seen her wearing the cat suit. But he had better things to do. "Roll over."

Slowly, seductively, she did exactly what he'd told her to.

Mairi had intended to tease Keir until they were both desperate for each other, but when she turned to look at him, she realized all she wanted was to have him close. To feel him inside her. To feel complete, instead of empty, just for one night.

She lay on her back, in the middle of his bed, and held out her hand to him. "Come make love to me."

Keir closed his eyes slowly, as though savoring her demand, and then he pulled his t-shirt over his head and tossed it away. A second later, he'd fished a condom out of his jeans, kicked off his shoes and stripped everything else off. He was magnificent as he slowly crawled up the bed to lie on his side next to her.

In his eyes, she could see words he wanted to say, but felt he couldn't. Words she wasn't ready to hear, might never be ready to hear. All Mairi could do was cup his nape and pull him down to her. His kiss was slow, sweet, almost reverential, and it was exactly what she needed. As their tongues met in a lazy dance, Keir's hand trailed over her body, caressing her breasts and tracing circles on her stomach until he reached the ache between her legs. An ache only Keir could assuage.

With a leg over hers, he widened her thighs and traced her sensitive lips with featherlight touches. Mairi clasped his shoulders, pulling him closer, needing to feel his strength against her. With a gasp for air, he broke their kiss and moved his lips to her throat, all the while tracing her clit with a teasing touch that drove her wild. She needed. There was no other word for it, only stark, desperate need.

"Keir," she gasped. "Please."

She expected him to joke about her lack of patience, but instead he leaned over her and stared into her eyes as his teasing fingers stilled. She watched as he started to say something, something he could never take back, and she pressed a finger to his lips.

"Later," she whispered, begging him to let her have this moment without the pressure of the past, or worry for the future, crushing her.

He let out a curse and slammed his mouth on hers, the kiss turning ferocious as his fingers plunged inside her. And just like that, Mairi shot up into the stratosphere and exploded. Panting and clinging to him, she felt him spread her legs to make room for his hips. She opened her eyes and leaned forward to trace the red swirls over his heart with the tip of her tongue. She wanted to memorize every line, in case it was the last time she saw them.

With a grunt, Keir plunged into her, and Mairi's head fell back. Her neck arched, and her legs wrapped around his thighs.

"Yes!" She dug her fingers into his shoulders and held on tight.

"You make me crazy," he growled against her throat,

giving her his weight as he slid in and out of her blissfully happy girl parts.

Mairi bit his shoulder and ran her tongue over the sting. He tasted musky and clean and smelled like warm sheets straight from the dryer. She wanted to wrap herself in him and never come out. A safe haven from the world. And that thought, that need, scared the life out of her. He was inside her, under her skin, burrowed deep, as she suspected he had been all along. She would never be done with Keir, and part of her never wanted to be.

As he took her away from herself, Mairi let her mind float on the sea of sensation he created. Aware only of Keir and what he made her feel. Aware of the desperate explosion building inside of her that he alone controlled. As they fell over the edge of sanity together, Mairi realized just how much she'd missed Keir's touch and wondered if she'd ever be able to give it up again..

For long minutes, she clung to him as they gasped for air. His weight was a comforting blanket and his heat seeped into her through her pores. She almost sobbed when he kissed her and headed for the bathroom, leaving the bed cold and empty without him. A minute later, he returned, turned off the lights and climbed in behind her. With an arm over her stomach and a leg thrown over her legs, he pinned her tight against him, his front to her back.

"Go to sleep, Rusty. Things will be better in the morning." He kissed her temple and curled a hand around her breast, as though he possessed it.

Mairi didn't sleep. She lay there, watching the shadows play over the walls and listening to Keir breathe behind her. The rhythm of his chest rising and falling was soothing to her. The heat from his body wrapped around her, keeping out the cold of life. A while later, he turned over and away from her, allowing her the chance to slip out of bed.

Stealing a blanket, she tiptoed down the stairs and curled up on the couch to think.

And that was where Keir found her hours later.

"Rusty, wake up." His gentle voice roused her, and she blinked up at him.

The light from the unadorned windows was stark, illuminating everything she had to deal with that day. Keir was dressed and crouched beside her. He gently brushed her hair from her face.

"What are you doing down here?" he asked.

"Was thinking."

His smile was gentle. "You come to any conclusions?"

"Aye." She tried to swallow, but her mouth was dry. "I'm going to take you up on your offer. I'm going to marry you, and I plan to tell everyone about it at a press conference tonight."

Keir's hand stilled on her hair. "You sure?"

"It's my only choice. You're right—my back is against the wall and I need you."

The light in his eyes dimmed somewhat. "Good decision." He stood and walked toward the door. "I'm making coffee. I've put a t-shirt on the bed for you, and your shorts are still good. Once you've had some breakfast, I'll take you home."

And then he was gone. Leaving Mairi alone to wonder what she'd just done.

CHAPTER 22

The minute Mairi told Keir she planned to take him up on his offer of marriage, he knew it was a mistake. He'd honestly thought he would take Mairi on any terms he could get her, but he'd discovered he was wrong.

Once he'd dropped her off at her apartment, which was still surrounded by news crews, onlookers, and fake boyfriends, Keir told Hamish he was on his own for the day and then rode to his brother's place in the middle of Campbeltown.

"Do you realize how early it is?" Sean said as he swung his door wide.

Keir stalked inside and headed straight for the kitchen, which was at the back of Sean's second-story apartment. "It's eight."

"Like I said, do you realize how early it is?"

"I'll make coffee." Keir reached for the pot.

"Then I forgive you. Now what the hell is wrong?" Sean slumped at the tiny two-person table in the corner of his equally tiny kitchen.

Keir purposely kept his back to his brother while he filled

the coffee machine, because he really didn't want to see his reaction. "Mairi's taking me up on my offer to get married."

There was silence. Keir carried on, spooning coffee into the pot and waiting for a reaction. Once he'd switched the machine on, he turned around to find Sean was no longer half-asleep.

"This is good, right?" Sean ran a hand through his hair, making it stand on end. "I mean, this is what you wanted."

Keir leaned back against the sink and rubbed his hands over his face. What a bloody mess.

"I thought it was what I wanted. I thought I'd be happy to take Mairi any way I could get her. Turns out I was an idiot. She doesn't love me. She made that clear when she said she'd marry me. I don't think she'll ever love me again."

Once the words were out, he turned away, and took mugs from the cupboard above the coffee maker. The pain in his chest was getting worse by the minute, and he rubbed the spot over his heart. The spot that was being torn in two.

"She literally said, 'I don't love you'?" Sean sounded somewhere between panicked and incredulous.

"No, she said she had no choice, that her back was against the wall. She's marrying me because she has no other option. It isn't like she has the money to run off and start again somewhere else." Keir took a breath and looked out of Sean's kitchen window over the rooftops of Campbeltown to the boats in the harbor. "Marrying her now will mean she'll always resent me. It will ruin any chance I have of getting her to love me again." He snorted. "Even if I had a chance to begin with."

"You're talking mad now. Of course you have a chance. You just fell for the world's most stubborn woman. You can't expect it to be easy. This is Mairi we're talking about. Nothing is easy with that woman."

Keir turned back to face his brother. "I don't know. I'm not sure it's possible to get past the damage I did to her."

Damage that had taken her out of his bed in the middle of the night, because she'd rather sleep alone on the sofa. Keir had woken in a panic, thinking she was gone. Instead, he'd found her curled in a ball, looking broken and bruised, as she told him she'd marry him.

"I can't do this," Keir said. "I can't hurt her again." He pushed away from the bench. "I'm taking off for a few days. I need you to explain to Mairi that it's for the best. She doesn't really want to marry me anyway."

"Are you insane?" Sean shouted, and crossed the distance between them.

For a moment, Keir thought Sean was going to try to shake some sense into him.

"You can't head off for a few days. That's exactly what you did last time. You left her when things got intense."

"Not by choice," Keir pointed out.

"Like she'd see the difference." Sean clasped handfuls of his hair. "Look. You need to stay. You need to see this out. You'll never get her back if you leave."

"I can't marry her, not like this. Not when she doesn't love me. I can't do that to either of us. I'm not running away. I just need a few days to think things through and regroup. I've got her into bed—that's further than I thought I'd get with her—but I can't marry her. Not when she's doing it under duress. What I need to do is slow things down, get her used to being with me again, without this marriage thing hanging over her head." He nodded. "It's for the best. I can't marry her like this."

"You stubborn bastard. Put your hurt feelings in a box and man the hell up. You can't back out now, not when she's told you she's willing to marry you. It's taken months to get to this stage. I didn't set this whole thing up to give you a chance at the woman, just so you could get all noble and bail at the first bloody setback."

Keir stilled. "You what?"

Sean's eyes went wide, and the color drained from his face. "Oh crap."

Keir stepped into his brother's space. "You set this up?"

His mind raced. This was just the sort of dumb thing Sean would do. He had the computer skills. Hell, he had a degree in computer design and spent his life setting up websites for people all over the world. On top of that, he was carrying around a ton of guilt over being the reason Keir went to jail and blew his relationship with Mairi. Of course he'd done this.

The interfering bastard.

Keir pulled back his arm, made a fist and punched his little brother right on the jaw. It was very satisfying.

Sean staggered back, clutched his face and glared at Keir. "I'm giving you that, because I probably deserve it. But you hit me again and I'm hitting back. Arsehole." He stalked to the freezer, pulled out a bag of peas and held it to his chin. "Feel better?"

"Not much." Keir folded his arms. "Tell me everything."

Mairi found Agnes sitting at the dining table with the laptop open on a hotel staff recruitment site.

"Am I Mum?" Mairi said as she plopped down into a chair beside her sister.

"What are you talking about now?" Agnes sat back in her chair and folded her arms.

"Logic, that's what I'm talking about." Mairi reached for the nearest box of chocolates and ripped into them. "There are four of us—odds are that one of us will take after Mum. I want to know if it's me."

Agnes rolled her eyes before helping herself to a chocolate. "Yes, it has to be you. It couldn't possibly be the sister who can't say no to anyone—just like Mum."

"Oh, I never thought of that. But..." Mairi bit into a caramel, and then tossed it at the bin. Caramels were only eaten when you didn't have anything else to eat, and her living room was full of chocolate, which meant she didn't have to waste time on caramels. "Am I Mum like she is with Dad?"

"Do you mean her going back for more when he treats her like crap, or her making excuses for everything he does?"

"Both." Mairi focused on the chocolates because she wasn't sure she wanted to hear the answer. Whatever it was, Agnes would give her the brutal truth.

"Honey." Agnes covered Mairi's hand with hers. "You're nothing like Mum. And Keir is nothing like Dad. Keir made *one* mistake with you, years ago. If you want to try again, then that's perfectly okay. It doesn't turn you into Mum."

Mairi looked at her sister and saw only understanding in Agnes' eyes. "What if he does it again?"

"He's highly unlikely to run out and steal a car while he's in bed with you. I think he learned his lesson."

Mairi ignored the sarcasm and gave her sister the truth: "I think I'm falling in love with him all over again."

"Oh, you precious child, you. You never stopped loving Keir. You've just been in a really, really bad mood with him for the past six years."

As soon as Agnes said the words, Mairi felt something fall into place inside her. It was true. She'd never stopped loving Keir. That was why that horrible night still hurt like hell.

"I don't know if I can ever trust him again," she confessed.

"Trust doesn't happen just because you decide it should, but you need to think about how Keir's behaved since he got out of prison. Heck, how he was before that night, too. I don't know what happened that night, but it was completely out of character for him. Sure, he was wild when he was a kid, but look at him now—he runs a successful business, people rely on him and he's known for stepping in to help when it's needed. Maybe all of that outweighs the other stuff. That's for you to decide."

Agnes wasn't saying anything that hadn't already occurred to Mairi. "I want to marry him," she blurted. "And not just because I have to. I've wanted him to be mine since I first saw him."

"I know." Agnes smiled and squeezed Mairi's hand.

Whatever else she was going to say was lost when the door down to the garage burst open and a furious Keir strode in, followed by a pale and sheepish Sean.

"Tell them what you told me," Keir said, batting the balloons that were still hovering at the ceiling out of his way.

Mairi sat up straight, the chocolate forgotten, as the obvious seriousness of the situation hit her.

"What is it?" she asked Keir. "Jonas is okay, right?"

His face softened. "Jonas is fine, but this idiot's life is in the balance. Talk." He smacked his brother's shoulder.

"Give me a chance, then," Sean snapped.

He took a deep breath and stepped back, putting a bit more space between him and the sisters, which made Mairi's hair stand on end. This wasn't going to be good. Not. At. All.

"Okay," Sean said. "I'm the one who hacked you. It was my idea."

Mairi froze, and Agnes let out a threatening little rumble that made Sean pale further. He shared a look with his brother, one that was particularly threatening on Keir's part.

"Why?" Mairi said.

Keir's threatening look got about a million times darker,

and Sean swallowed hard. "No reason. Just thought it would be fun."

And Mairi snapped.

One second she was sitting there with chocolates on her lap, the next she was hanging off Sean's back, with her arm around his throat, trying to choke the life out of him.

"I'm going to kill you," Mairi shouted. "I'm going to chop you into pieces and put them on stakes outside in the street to warn off the next idiot who thinks it might be fun to mess with me."

Sean staggered around the room, tripping over chocolates and flowers, popping balloons and getting tangled in ribbon —all while Mairi was attached to his back.

"Someone get her off me," he whined.

He sounded strangled. That was good. Because strangled was exactly what she was aiming for. If his hair had been longer, and she could have gotten a decent grip, she would have pulled that out too, just for good measure.

"You ruined my life," she shouted. "You deserve death."

"Get her off!"

Mairi tightened her grip.

"I'm dying. I can't breathe," Sean shouted, proving he could breathe and was just being a wimp.

A strong arm wrapped around Mairi's waist and another hand pried her arms from around Sean's throat. She kicked against Keir. "Let me at him. He deserves this."

"I agree." Keir held Mairi under his left arm, while he punched his brother's nose with his right fist.

"Is anyone going to listen to me if I tell you violence isn't the answer?" Agnes said from the table.

"No!" Keir and Mairi shouted.

"That's it," Sean said, while he held his nose with one hand and rubbed his neck with the other. "I don't deserve this. I'm telling her—"

He didn't get a chance to finish, because Keir dropped Mairi to the floor, grabbed his brother by the back of his shirt and threw him out the door, slamming it firmly behind him.

"Tell me what?" Mairi said.

"Nothing. He's just being a moron." He folded his arms, making his biceps bulge, and looked immovable.

Mairi wasn't going to get any further explanation out of him.

"I hope you two are going to clean up the mess you made," Agnes said.

Mairi looked down, and sure enough, the floor was littered with mashed chocolates, trampled flowers and burst balloons.

"It looks like Valentine's Day has been massacred in our living room," Mairi said.

"I'm sorry, Rusty," Keir said. "If I'd known it was him, I'd have stopped everything."

"I know." She looked at his impossibly handsome face. "Will he tell everyone at the meeting tonight?"

"I'll make sure he does."

She toed some of the trampled flowers to avoid looking him in the eye. "I guess this means we don't have to get married, then."

"No. You don't have to marry me. You've been saved from that." His voice was completely flat, giving nothing away.

"Well, that's good, isn't it?" She looked at him but couldn't read anything from his face. It was closed up tight.

"Aye. It's good. It's what you wanted."

"Yeah," Mairi said softly.

They stared into each other's eyes for the longest time, and Mairi saw pain in Keir's, maybe some regret—but worst of all, she saw resignation.

At last, he cleared his throat. "Okay, I'll go sort out Sean." And then he was gone, closing the door firmly behind him.

Mairi stood there, staring after him until Agnes walked in front of her. She held up a glass full of water and threw the contents in Mairi's face.

"What the hell, Agnes?"

"I thought you needed waking up." Agnes glared at her. "You want him. He wants you. This is painful to watch. Get a grip, pull up your big girl knickers and sort this out. You think that man is going to hang around here waiting for you forever? He isn't. Not if he thinks you still hate his guts. Stop letting your fear rule you, or you're going to lose him. Is that what you want? On top of that, the rest of us are fed up with you two circling each other. It's making us nauseated."

She stalked away, leaving Mairi to drip onto the debris-strewn carpet.

CHAPTER 23

The meeting took place on the green outside Edna's shop. Under Agnes' instruction, Keir and the fake boyfriends put together a small stage in front of the cliff. Seeing as Mairi would be using it, they built it far enough away from the edge not to be a danger. They rigged up a microphone and a large screen with a projector aimed at it—because Mairi had insisted that Sean give his confession in a bullet-point presentation format her guys would understand.

Not that Keir had seen Mairi since he'd dragged his brother into her flat. According to Agnes, she'd needed the time to plan what she was going to say at the meeting. Knowing how little thought Mairi put into everything she did, Keir suspected she was just napping.

"Are you going to hit me again if I talk to you?" Sean asked as he came up beside him.

"Depends on whether something really dumb comes out of your mouth."

"I wanted to check that you weren't still planning on running away."

"Yeah, there's a good chance you're going to get hit again.

I don't run. I never run. And I'm definitely not running now that I've managed to get Mairi in my bed. I'm going to hang around and wear her down with great sex, until she realizes she loves me and has to marry me for real."

"Good plan. How long do you think that will take?"

"The way Mairi holds a grudge? Five, maybe six years."

"You two have a seriously twisted relationship, you know that, right?"

"Aye." Keir grinned with pride.

Behind him, the grass had filled with people who'd come from far and wide to witness Mairi's announcement about whom she'd picked to wed. They were going to be disappointed. Which made Keir want to cackle with depraved laughter.

Two news crews had set up near the front of the crowd. They'd been joined by two other crews, from the main morning TV shows. A food truck was parked in the far corner, ready to sell hot pies and chips to the masses. Over the road, Edna's shop was doing a roaring trade, and the woman was actually happy for once.

The night was mild, and the sky was clear, making it easy to see the carpet of stars above, and if you concentrated hard, and listened beyond the chatter of the crowd, you could hear the waves lapping at the base of the cliff. It was a perfect night for Mairi to put an end to this mess.

Keir and Sean stood at the edge of the stage while the geeks tweaked the sound system and computer setup they'd rigged up for Sean's confession As Keir watched, a ripple started at the back of the crowd and grew as it edged toward the front—Mairi was coming.

The crowd parted in front of him and he saw her clearly. She was wearing curve-hugging jeans, a black t-shirt with *Can't Tie Me Down* in white letters across her chest and a pair of well-worn cowboy boots she'd owned for years. Her hair was wild around her shoulders and her lips were painted pink. She took his breath away and made his head spin.

Mairi walked straight up to him and smiled wide. "We ready to start?"

"Aye." He nodded to the t-shirt. "Subtle."

"I thought so." She pushed her shoulders back and stared him in the eye. "You going to be here when this is over?"

"Rusty, you couldn't drag me away. We have things we need to settle."

"Not settle," Mairi said with a sparkle in her eye. "Explore."

That one word made his knees weak, and he almost crumpled to the ground before he locked them in place. There was no time to answer her, to ask what she meant, because she was already climbing onto the stage. The lights came on, and there she was, in the spotlight— with the vast, dark sky as a backdrop.

"I won't say thanks for coming," Mairi said into the microphone, "because I'd have preferred it if you'd all stayed home and minded your own business."

There was laughter. That was the Scots for you—insults rolled off them like water.

"As you know, a week or so ago, the Girlfriend website was hacked, and a message appeared telling my online boyfriends that I wanted a husband."

There was a cheer, and Mairi waited for it to pass.

"You guys just glossed right over the word 'hacked,' didn't you?" More laughter, and she shook her head. "Anyway, I don't want a husband. I didn't post that message, but I do have the person who did. Sean, get up here."

Sean looked at the crowd and turned green.

"Don't make me hit you again," Keir told his brother.

"I'm telling Mum on you," was Sean's very mature reply.

Sean climbed onto the stage and stood beside Mairi,

looking like he'd rather have had a root canal at the same time as a colonoscopy.

"This is Sean," Mairi said with a smile. "He's the idiot who thought it would be fun to hack my site, and he's here to explain how he did it, in a way that will make you lot believe him. If you listen carefully to his convoluted and technical explanation, I'll have some fun things to tell you after he's done." She smacked him on the back—with force. "Get on with it."

Sean tapped his laptop keyboard, and the screen behind him filled with an image of Mairi's Girlfriend page. That's as far as Keir got before he tuned his brother out. Instead, he watched the geek boys as they listened to the explanation and saw the moment they believed Sean had done it, their faces filled with shock, disappointment and then anger. Sean had made no friends in this crowd.

When Sean was done, Mairi took the mic back from him. "There it is. I'm truly sorry for the misunderstanding." She looked down at her men. "I'm especially sorry to you guys, because I have no intention of marrying any of you. That doesn't mean you aren't great guys. I want all of you to come up here, because I have something I need to say to the world." She looked over at the morning TV reporter. "You'll record all of this for the show, right?"

He gave her a thumbs-up.

The men shuffled onto the stage behind Mairi, their shoulders slumped. The sight made Keir feel sorry for them. Their faces were flushed, and they were clearly embarrassed that they'd fallen for Sean's lies, and now the world would know how dumb they'd been.

"Are you sure about this, Mairi?" one of the guys asked. "We could still woo you and see where it goes."

She shook her head and then took the microphone off the

stand. She held it close to those perfect lips. "I'm having sex with Keir."

Keir staggered back a step as all eyes turned to him. Yeah, he hadn't been expecting Mairi to broadcast that little tidbit.

"Is this the kind of situation where you try something before you buy?" one of the other guys asked. "Are you going to have sex with all of us?"

"What? No!" Mairi glared at him. "I'd expect better from you, Raymond." She turned to the crowd. "I want to make this clear right now. I am only having sex with Keir. I've only ever had sex with Keir, and I intend to keep on doing it—solely with Keir."

Keir lost the ability to breathe as a cheer went up. His brother patted him on the back.

"Guess hacking her site was worth it after all," Sean said.

"Don't think that lets you off the hook," Keir said through his shock, and Sean looked miserable again.

"Typical," John, one of Mairi's guys, said. "You're having sex with the guy with abs and no brain. That's why we don't have a chance. Women always go for looks over substance."

Keir took a step toward the stage, his fists clenched. He'd had just about enough of these guys. Sean put a hand on his arm to stop him. "Don't punch a geek in front of the cameras."

"That's not true," Mairi said. "Darius and Damien have abs, and I'm not sleeping with them."

"It's true. We have great abs," Darius said, then he elbowed his brother and they both flashed their abs to the crowd, who catcalled and whistled.

"Is this going to turn into a *Full Monty* situation?" Sean said. "Because I really don't want to be here if it does."

"We're getting off track," Mairi said. "I'm not getting married to any of my online boyfriends, but that doesn't mean I don't care about each of them. In fact, they are some of the most amazing guys I've ever met, and I want to introduce you to them."

There was another cheer as Mairi called Amir forward. "This is Amir. He's from Pakistan and is a genius in genetic research. He's also pretty damn good at playing online poker, because he beats me all the time." She wrapped an arm around his waist and smiled up at the man who was only a few inches taller than her. "Amir took me on the most romantic date I've ever had, and I will never forget it. He is a kind, caring, loving man who deserves a woman who will appreciate everything about him."

Amir's face turned a deep red, and he clearly didn't know what to do with himself. The crowd clapped and whistled. Some chanted his name, and he started to laugh.

Mairi kissed his cheek and moved on to the twins. "This is Darius and Damien," she said. "Darius isn't looking for a wife just yet, but his brother Damien is. Damien is a programming genius who enjoys playing football, rock-climbing and kayaking. Damien and Darius saved my life this week when I fell over the cliff. They did it by rappelling down to me and bringing me back up. These guys are genuine heroes. So, if you're a woman who appreciates a hero with a big side order of geek, Damien is the guy for you."

As there was more applause, Keir felt a warmth spread through him. His woman was a genius.

"She's getting them wives," Sean said, sounding slightly awestruck.

"Aye, she is." Keir looked at her with pride.

"Come here, Sebastian." She grabbed the guy's hand and pulled him to the front of the stage. "This is Sebastian. He's from Canada and is an incredibly loyal friend, as well as a genius with artificial intelligence. I had to force Sebastian to be here tonight, because he didn't want to leave his friend alone in the hospital. Sebastian is sweet and funny and is able to translate Wookiee into English, which is a skill that might come in handier than you think."

There was laughter and whistles for Sebastian.

"Pass me the photo," she said to Sebastian, who handed her a large photo of Jonas, sans Wookiee mask. There were gasps from the women in the crowd at the sight of his model-perfect features. "This is Jonas. He couldn't be here tonight, because he suffered burns this week when he got too close to a firework display. Jonas suffers from debilitating shyness, but he is one of the most amazing men I've ever met. He's a programming savant who became a millionaire before he turned twenty. He is also fluent in Wookiee."

There was laughter.

"Where can I sign up for one of these guys?" a woman shouted.

"I want one too," someone else called out.

Mairi beamed at them. "You can sign up on the Mairi's Wedding Facebook page, which I now control." She shot a warning glare at Sean, who hurriedly gave her a thumbs-up. "I'll be working to find romantic partners for all my men, and I will be very strict in vetting any applicants, because these guys deserve only the best. Which, for the record, isn't me, but I can find it. I'm good at that."

Once the cheering settled, Mairi continued to list the attributes of each of her men, and her new business was born.

"She wants me to set up a website for her and maintain it," Sean grumbled. "I wondered why she needed one. Now I know. And she wants me to do it for free."

"It's the least you can do."

"I have to update the Girlfriend site as well—make their security ironclad and reimburse them for the revenue they lost."

"You really are a numpty." Keir didn't want to get into the details of his brother's idiotic idea. He was too busy watching his woman woo the crowd for her fake boyfriends. She'd been born to stand for these men. She was the best advocate they could ever have.

"It was worth it," Sean said with a grin. "She plans to keep having sex with you."

"Yes, she does." Keir flashed a wicked smile at the woman on stage, who flushed when she saw it.

"That's about it," Mairi said. "Except for Roberto. Roberto got lost riding his scooter into Glasgow. If anybody finds him, can you please mail him back to me?"

The crowd went wild and surged forward, swamping the men, asking for autographs and making them stutter and blush. Through the mass of people, Keir lost sight of Mairi.

"Can you wind this up and send everybody home?" he asked Sean. "I've got a woman to track down."

He pushed his way into the crowd, keeping an eye open for wild red hair.

CHAPTER 24

There was no sign of Mairi in the crowd, so Keir headed to the garage to see if she'd made it back to her apartment. That was when he found her. She was sitting astride his motorbike, just like she'd done the first time he'd ever set eyes on her. And just like then, he was pulled to her side by an invisible rope that tied them together, one that never faded and was impossible to break.

He prowled straight for her, her eyes heating as he got closer. At last, he stood in front of her, brushed her hair from her face and fought the urge to kiss her until they were both wild with need.

"Where are we going, Rusty?" he said.

"Wherever you want to take me," she answered.

"I want to take you everywhere."

"Okay," she whispered, never taking her eyes from him. "I have a confession."

"Yeah?" His heart stuttered, and he hoped this was a good confession, because he didn't think he could take one that came with disappointment. Not when she was finally looking at him without the fear that had lived in her eyes for far too long.

"I still love you," she said.

Keir breathed in her words, with his eyes closed, and his head bent forward. He'd spent years dreaming of hearing those words from her lips.

"I want to put the past behind us," she said. "I want to try again."

He shook his head, hardly believing this was real. "You destroy me," he whispered before he threaded his fingers into her hair and pulled her lips to his.

She tasted of strawberries and chocolate, and she sank into his embrace without a moment's hesitation. He kissed her long, hard, deep—stamping his possession on her mouth. Letting her know, through his kiss, that he was never letting her go. Never again. When they broke for air, he rested his forehead against hers.

"I have a confession of my own to make," he said.

"Yeah?" She slid her hands under his shirt and up his chest, distracting him with her sensual touch, until she caressed the tattoo that sat over his heart. "Does it have anything to do with this tattoo that looks suspiciously like curly red hair?"

He smiled and pressed a kiss to her nose. "You figured that out, did you?"

"It wasn't exactly subtle, babe."

His heart thrilled at the endearment, but he had to get rid of the last barrier between them. "I need to tell you about the night I left you."

"I don't need to hear it, Keir. I've thought about it and realized that I was too hurt and angry to notice something obvious about that night."

He stilled, hardly daring to breathe. "What was that?"

"That it was completely out of character for you. You

wouldn't have left me unless there was a good reason." She frowned. "It has something to do with whoever was in that car with you, doesn't it? The people you wouldn't sell out to the police."

"Aye, Rusty, it has a whole lot to do with them"—he took a deep breath—"and the fact I wasn't even in the car."

He watched realization dawn. "It was Sean. You took the blame for him. He was always in trouble back then. You stepped in to keep him from getting some serious jail time, didn't you?"

"Aye. I thought they would give me a rap on the knuckles and send me away, but they sent me to jail instead."

"Why didn't you tell me?"

"You were mad, gorgeous. Spitting mad. We couldn't trust that you wouldn't take our secret straight to the police. Then I'd have stayed locked up for lying under oath and perverting the course of justice, and my idiot brother would have done time too."

She huffed. "Okay, I'll give you that, because it's exactly what I would have done."

"I left you that night because I had to save my brother. I had to buy him a chance to get away from the losers he was hanging out with and turn his life around."

"And he did." She didn't sound happy about it, and he suspected that it would take his grudge-bearing redhead years to get past it.

"Aye, but you need to know I would never have left your bed for something less than that. Something less than life or death."

"He didn't die," Mairi said with a pout. "But I can fix that."

"Don't tempt me. Between that night and this mess with the hacking, I'm sorely tempted to put him out of his misery as well."

"Agnes says I stay angry for an unreasonably long time

and that I can't think rationally while I'm like that. There's a good chance I'll make Sean suffer for years. I feel I should tell you this, because of the whole brother love thing."

He wisely kept his mouth shut about her tendency to bear a grudge long term. "You should also know that he hacked your site and set up this whole husband competition to force the two of us together. He said we were stuck in a stalemate, and he wanted to make you notice me again."

That didn't make her look any happier. "Maybe we should wait until I calm down before we deal with Sean."

His lips twitched, but he had the good sense not to grin. "Great idea. How long do you think you need?"

"Ten years?"

"Sounds about right."

He reached for his spare helmet, the one he kept just for her, and strapped it on Mairi's head, all the while staring into her eyes. Eyes that told him she was his soul mate.

"Budge up," he said, and climbed on in front of her. He grabbed her hand and tugged her up against his back. "Hold on tight, Rusty. I'm going to take you for the ride of your life."

"I know."

And then she wrapped her arms around him, and they rode off into the night.

Together.

EPILOGUE

SIX MONTHS LATER

Mairi had taken over the downstairs bedroom in Keir's—no, *their*—house to use as her office. Her new business, matchmaking for geeks, had taken off with a bang. The publicity around the husband competition had brought lots of interested partners for her men straight to her new website. The news of the husband hack, as it was now being called, had spread all over the world, and interest in her new business was booming. Within weeks, she had more clients than she could cope with and had to take on staff—two of them. They worked part-time to help her sort through the thousands of women who'd gotten in touch about her geeks. In fact, things were going so well that she was thinking about branching out into finding men for female geeks. But that would have to wait until she she'd sorted out more matches first.

Mairi could hardly believe how things had turned around. She was a business owner. With staff. Sometimes she had to pinch herself to check it wasn't some weird dream and she'd wake to find herself naked in the middle of Campbeltown.

"You ready to go?"

Keir stood in the doorway to her office, which she'd painted pink and filled with plenty of bright blue cushions in her mission to bring color to Keir's life. He had his arms folded over another muscle shirt, which made his shoulders bulge. He did it on purpose because he knew his shoulders were a siren call to her. They derailed her at least twice a day.

"I'm ready."

She checked her briefcase, which held her laptop, tablet, phone, backup phone and several chargers. Just looking at it made her feel like an international executive. An executive who dressed in jeans, flip-flops and a red t-shirt with the words *Klingons do It on the Starboard Bow*. It had been a gift from Sebastian, who had a flair for finding cool shirts. He sent them to her regularly, whenever he came across one. Keir didn't mind that Sebastian sent her clothes, although he drew the line at her receiving anything from a sex shop. She flicked some fluff off the front of her shirt and fought the urge to check her phone again. Sebastian was on his second date with a woman from France, and Mairi was keeping her fingers crossed that this was the one. So far, she'd found matches for Amir and John. She was working on the rest of her men and had high hopes she would find them all perfect partners.

"If you don't get a move on, we're going to miss our flight," Keir said.

"Calm down, I'm ready. We can leave." She rolled her eyes at him.

She could hardly believe what they were about to do. Keir had bought them round-the-world tickets, and Mairi had managed to set up face-to-face meetings with some of her clients during their trip—which meant the trip was tax-deductible. That in itself said romance to a Scottish woman, but the fact they were going to see some of the places they'd talked about years earlier was what made it truly special.

One day, upstairs in the spare room, there would be a tiny bed with a little girl in it, who would listen to stories of her mother's adventures and plan her own life full of excitement.

As she reached Keir, he wrapped his arms around her and kissed her senseless. Something he'd had plenty of time to do since he'd sold his garage to his apprentice, Hamish. The plan was to start a new garage in Campbeltown once they got back from their trip.

"When are you going to marry me, Rusty?" Keir said when they came up for air.

"I keep telling you, proposals should be romantic, and they should be a question. Yelling 'marry me' while we're riding your bike is not a proposal."

"You're a hard woman to please," he said with a grin.

"It would probably be wise to remember that." She grabbed his hand and tugged him toward the door. "The bags are already in the car, right?"

"Everything is in the car, except us."

"I can't believe we're doing it." She grinned at him. "I can't believe we're travelling. It's going to be so much fun."

"You bet it is." His smile was perfection and warmed her heart.

Mairi threw their front door open and stopped dead. Their lawn was full of people, all of whom she recognized. Her geek boys were there, even Sebastian with the French girl at his side. The residents from the old folks' home were there, with Gladys in between her two men, as usual. Her sisters were there too—even her wonderful niece and nephew were grinning at her. All of them, the whole crowd, beamed at her. Then, as one, they held up cards that spelled out, *Say Yes, Say Yes, Say Yes...*

Mairi's mouth fell open as she turned to the grinning fool beside her. Only he wasn't where she'd left him. He was down on one knee.

"Rusty." He reached for her hand. "I'm on my knees because I'll beg if I have to. Will you marry me?"

"You remembered it's a question." Mairi felt like her heart was going to burst, it was so full.

She tugged him up and threw herself into his arms. They stumbled back into the hall, and Keir kicked the door closed on their cheering crowd.

"I didn't even get the ring out, but I'll take that as a yes," Keir said smugly before he kissed her.

"It's definitely a yes," Mairi said against his mouth.

And then they missed their flight.

AN EXCERPT FROM RAGE

Read on for a taste of Isobel's story.

Isobel Sinclair should have contacted the authorities the first time she saw the boat sneaking into the cove. But she didn't. She should have called when there was a storm during the boat's third visit, and the crew lost some of their baggage on the rocky path up to Arness. But she didn't. Instead, she'd gathered their lost cargo, called it her own and sold it to help pay off her ex-husband's debts.

Which made her a thief, just like him.

And her thieving was the reason she still didn't call in the authorities the time the boat turned up in the dead of night, and there was shouting in the darkness. Or the time she'd seen evidence that someone had dragged something heavy over the beach.

No, she'd never called the authorities. Not once. Even though she knew the boat brought nothing but trouble each time it snuck into shore.

But she should have called, because the boat had come back.

And this time, they'd left a body behind.

"What are we going to do with him?" Isobel's youngest sister, Mairi, stared down at the man.

The dead man.

"I suppose we could bury him," Agnes, one of their middle sisters, said.

"We can't bury him here." Isobel gestured to the rock-strewn beach. "Even if we do manage to dig a hole, the tide will unearth him in a day or two."

Mairi looked up at the steep, rocky path behind them, the only route down from the bluff where the tiny town of Arness sat. "We'll never get him back up there. He looks like he weighs a ton."

"And he's wet." Agnes nodded. "That makes you heavier."

"Aye," Mairi said. "Water retention."

Isobel and Agnes stared at their sister.

"What?" Mairi said.

With shakes of their heads, Agnes and Isobel turned their attention back to the body.

"How do you think he died?" Agnes said.

"I suppose we should look him over and see if we can tell." Isobel didn't like the thought of touching the man, let alone examining him for clues as to his cause of death.

"Does it really matter how he died?" Mairi said. "I mean, it isn't going to change the fact that he's dead. Or that he was left here by the boat people."

"The boat people?" Agnes looked towards heaven and seemed to be counting to ten. Again.

Mairi shrugged, her long red hair shifting with the movement. "What else are we to call them? And he *was* left here by the boat crew. Isobel saw them while she was spying."

Isobel adopted her patented "haughty eldest sister" look—it helped take her mind off her shaking hands and the fear gnawing at her stomach. "I wasn't spying. I was looking out of my window and saw them carry him off the boat and dump him here."

"You were looking out of your window with the aid of binoculars," Mairi reminded her.

She had a point. "What I don't get is if these *boat people* are so keen on going unnoticed, then why are they dumping bodies on the beach?" Isobel said. "I mean, they only come in the dead of night. And we know they're up to no good."

"Smuggling," Mairi said with a decisive nod.

Agnes walked around the prone man and looked back out at the choppy waters behind them, then up at the hill leading to town. "Do you think they meant for him to be swept out to sea? Or to be eaten by the crabs?"

"If they wanted him to be swept out to sea, why not dump him out there in the first place?" Isobel said. "And I don't think half a dozen crabs are enough to eat a full-grown body. At least not fast enough to get rid of the evidence."

"Even then," Mairi said, "there would still be the bones."

They nodded in agreement, and Isobel couldn't help but notice that her sisters were struggling to hide their shaking hands, just as she was doing.

"I think we should call the police." Seeing as Agnes wasn't the most law-abiding member of the family, it said a lot that she was the one to suggest calling them in.

"I can't." Isobel tugged at the sleeves of her oversized purple cardigan and wrapped her arms around herself. "They'll find out that I sold the stuff I found, rather than reporting it to them in the first place."

"I told you, you shouldn't have gone to the pawn shop in Campbeltown," Mairi said. "Too many people know us there."

"I wanted rid of it fast."

Plus, she'd needed the money to pay off the loan shark who was hounding her over her ex-husband's debt. Seeing as the man couldn't find Robert, he'd decided to make Isobel pay in his stead, with cash or her body, making it clear that her family would suffer if she didn't comply. That was the reason Isobel's moral judgment had been silenced when she'd found the stolen goods on the path—the thought of handing over her body to pay her ex-husband's debt made her ill. But she'd do it if she had to. She'd do just about anything to make sure her kids were safe.

"Enough of this." Agnes crouched down and turned the body over.

He flopped onto his back, and the cause of death was instantly clear. There was a wide, gaping slit where his throat used to be.

"I think I'm going to be sick." Mairi covered her mouth and turned her back on the body, making gagging sounds as she did so.

"Don't," Agnes ordered. "You know I'm a sympathetic puker. If you start vomiting, we'll both be doing it."

Isobel ignored her sisters as she stared at the body. It was the most horrifying thing she'd ever seen. She swallowed hard. "You can't accidentally slit your own throat, can you?"

"No," Agnes said firmly.

Aye, that would have been too much to hope for.

There was a scrambling noise from the bluff behind them. The women yelped and spun, to see their remaining sister coming down the rocky path.

Isobel put her hand to her chest. Her heart was racing hard. "You nearly gave me a heart attack," she told her sister.

Donna rushed up to them, her blonde hair flying out behind her. "Sorry. What's so urgent we had to meet in the dark on the beach? Did you find more bounty?"

It was then she saw the body. The colour drained from her face, she turned and promptly vomited. Which, in turn, made Agnes vomit.

Mairi started making gagging noises. "I'm okay, I'm okay." She held one hand up, pressing the other to her stomach. "I can hold it."

"What a relief," Isobel told her.

Mairi shot her an irritated look. "I told you not to call Donna. She's vegetarian."

"I didn't expect her to eat him." Isobel glared back at her.

"That's just gross," Mairi said, and gagged again.

Isobel threw her hands up in disgust. "Why did I bother calling any of you? You're no use at all. We have a situation here and all you're doing is being sick."

"It's not like we can help it," Agnes said, looking decidedly green.

"Some warning would have been good." Donna swayed in place. Her eyes were on the water instead of the man.

"I did warn you when I called," Isobel said through gritted teeth. "I said, come quick, there's a dead body on the beach."

"I thought you were joking," Donna said.

"About a dead body?" Isobel practically shrieked.

"Right." Agnes held up her hands. "Everybody calm down. This isn't helping. It's getting light, and we need to deal with the body. It's not like people use this beach, but if someone did come down here, they'd call the police." She looked at Isobel. "And seeing as your house is the closest, you'd be first on their list to interview."

"That wouldn't go well," Mairi said. "Your whole face goes red when you lie, and you start stuttering."

"Then you just blab the truth and apologise for trying to lie," Donna added.

"Which means you'd get arrested for fencing stolen goods." Agnes nodded. "Something we're trying to avoid."

"Are you all about done?" Isobel put her hands on her hips and glared at them. Was this really the time to bring up every single one of her flaws? "The kids will be awake soon. We need to deal with this now."

They all stared at the man.

"I've never seen a dead body before," Mairi said. "They look so lifeless."

"Idiot." Agnes smacked Mairi on the back of the head.

"What was that for?" Mairi rubbed her head.

"For being an idiot," Agnes said. "Now focus. Do we leave him here? Cover him and come back later to bury him? Bury him now? Or move him somewhere else while we think things over?"

"I think we need to move him. It would be too hard to bury him here, and we couldn't guarantee the tide wouldn't unearth him later." Isobel felt weary. She was sick of the stress in her life. Sick of dealing with other people's messes. Sick of struggling every single day just to survive. "Whatever we do, we need to do it fast, before the kids wake up. Either way, I want him off the beach. Jack sometimes comes down here with his friends after school, and I wouldn't want them to find the body."

"You could put him in the freezer in your garage," Donna said. "It still works, doesn't it?"

"Aye, but it's old, full of rust and smelly," Isobel said.

"I don't think he'll care," Donna said.

"What do we do with him once he's in the freezer? We can't leave him there forever." Isobel gnawed at her bottom lip and wondered how her life had come to this point.

She was a single mother of two, with two failed relationships behind her, a mountain of debt she hadn't personally accumulated, a minimum-wage job in the village shop and an ever-growing list of crimes under her belt. It was not how she'd imagined life would be at the grand old age of thirty-two.

"We need advice. We need someone who knows what to do with a dead body," Agnes said. "We need an expert."

"I'm not calling the police," Isobel said adamantly. She was the only stability her kids had. She couldn't even think of risking it.

"I wasn't thinking of the police," Agnes said. "I was thinking of an outlaw."

"Yes!" Mairi clapped her hands and grinned. "Great idea, Aggie."

"No." Isobel shook her head. "No. Just no."

Donna placed her hand on Isobel's arm. "Don't dismiss this idea just because you fancy the man. He used to be in the army. He's bound to have seen dead bodies during conflict. He must have an idea what to do with them."

"I-I don't f-fancy him," Isobel protested, but nobody was listening. No, she just dreamed about him every blooming night. What was it with her and bad boys? Hadn't she learned her lesson by now? Why couldn't she find a nice six-stone weakling of an accountant to fall in love with?

"It's well known he's dangerous," Agnes said. "Old man McKay used to tell everyone that his grandson was deadly. He was in the Special Forces. He knows about dead bodies."

"Plus," Mairi said, "there's a security company watching him—*covertly*." She whispered the last word as though it had special powers. "That must mean he's on the other side of the law now, which means he won't report us to the cops."

"I didn't know he was being watched." Donna's eyes went wide. "Maybe talking to him isn't such a good idea."

"I spoke to the woman who was setting up cameras," Isobel said. Of course she was going to grill a stranger who was setting up CCTV in the street, in the dark. "She showed me her ID and said he wasn't dangerous to the town. He isn't a criminal. She said he's only dangerous to bad guys." And then the blue-haired woman had laughed. It wasn't reassuring. Neither was the fact she was wearing a Wonder Woman T-shirt and a pair of pink, glittery Doc Marten boots. "She gave me her business card, in case I was ever worried about anything."

"Maybe we should call the security company instead?" Mairi said. "We can ask them what to do."

Agnes groaned. "I can just imagine that conversation— 'Hello, we have the body of a stranger in our freezer and we're looking for suggestions on what to do with it.' Aye, that would go well."

"It was only an idea." Mairi frowned at Agnes.

"Whatever," Agnes said. "I think our best bet is the outlaw. You said he's huge and there are weapons lying around in his house. He's obviously used to dangerous situations. I bet he'd know what to do with the body. You need to ask him for help."

"No."

Isobel had been delivering groceries to Callum McKay's house for almost four months, and she'd only seen the man three times. All three times, he'd scared the life out of her. Rage covered him like a shroud. But there was also something about him that made her heart ache. Maybe it was the utter desolation in his eyes, or the fact that the only people she'd seen near him had been from a security company that was hiding in the dark. She'd never met someone so completely alone. And so brutally raw. He was the embodiment of her own personal weakness—the tortured bad boy, with muscles like Thor. She didn't have to be massively self-aware to realise that he was the *last* person she should approach for help. No, for the sake of her sanity, it was best to keep far, far away from the man.

"Honey," Agnes said, "we don't have a lot of options here. Either you get help from someone who knows what to do with a body, or you keep the guy frozen in your old chest freezer for the foreseeable future."

"Aye," Donna said. "And what if this is just the beginning? What if the boat people dump more bodies? We need a plan. We need advice."

"Or we need to start our own crematorium business," Mairi said.

"Think of your kids," Agnes said. "This is getting worse every month. We're in way over our heads. We need help. If this guy can help, then great. If not, we'll try something else."

Isobel's heart sank. Agnes was right. They were out of options. Staying away from Callum McKay had become a luxury she couldn't afford. And it wasn't as if she wanted to start a relationship with him. No, she just wanted advice on what to do with the dead stranger who'd been dumped on her beach.

"You can do it," Donna said softly. "We have your back."

Isobel blinked back tears, as love for her sisters overwhelmed her. She didn't know how she'd survive without them. She needed to talk to Callum for their sakes. This situation with the mysterious boat was well past the point of being dangerous, and they were getting in deeper every month. No, *they* weren't —*she* was. And she was dragging her sisters down with her.

"Okay, I'll talk to him."

"You'll be okay, honey," Agnes said.

"Just keep your hands off him," Mairi said. "Maybe you could call him instead of talking to him face to face."

That caused Agnes to smack her again. "She isn't going to jump the man, idiot."

There was a pause as all three sisters gave her speculative looks. Isobel threw up her hands in disgust. "So I have a type. So what? It's not like I'm going to throw myself at him and offer to sleep with him in return for his help."

There was a shuffling of feet as her sisters cast sideward glances at each other.

"Thanks a lot," Isobel said. "Good to know you have so much faith in me."

"You tend to get physical without thinking it through," Donna said gently.

"I only did that once," Isobel protested. And ended up pregnant and alone at seventeen because of it.

Her sisters stared at her.

"Fine. Twice." And she had the ex-husband from hell to show for that little slip in self-control.

"If it's any consolation," Mairi said, "I've totally learned from your mistakes."

"No. It's no consolation. Now do you three think you could stop analysing my past mistakes long enough to help me get this body off the beach?" She looked at the sliver of light on the horizon. "Sun's coming. We need to get him to the garage and into the freezer before the kids wake up."

"This is going to be gross," Mairi said. "I'll need to burn my clothes after this."

"I might vomit again," Donna said.

"Get a grip," Agnes snapped, "and take an arm or a leg each."

With each of them clutching a limb, the four sisters carried the dead man up the hill to Isobel's house. Donna and Agnes were only sick twice.

Get Rage now to keep on reading!

ABOUT THE AUTHOR

I'm a Scot, living in New Zealand and married to a Dutch man. I write contemporary romance with a humorous bent – this is mainly due to the fact I have an odd sense of humour and can't keep it out of anything I do! If I wasn't a writer, I'd like to be Buffy the Vampire Slayer, or Indiana Jones. Unfortunately, both these roles have already been filled. Which may be a good thing as I have no fighting skills, wouldn't know a precious relic if it hit me in the face and have an aversion to blood. When I'm not living in my head, I'm a mother to two kids, several pet sheep, one dog, four cats, three alpacas, two miniature horses, eight guinea pigs and an escape artist chicken.